storm
warning

NIV Faithgirlz!™ Backpack Bible
My Faithgirlz!™ Journal

Blog On series

Grace Notes (Book One)
Love, Annie (Book Two)
Just Jazz (Book Three)
Storm Rising (Book Four)
Grace Under Pressure (Book Five)
Upsetting Annie (Book Six)
Jazz Off-Key (Book Seven)

Sophie series

Sophie's World (Book One)
Sophie's Secret (Book Two)
Sophie and the Scoundrels (Book Three)
Sophie's Irish Showdown (Book Four)
Sophie's First Dance? (Book Five)
Sophie's Stormy Summer (Book Six)
Sophie Breaks the Code (Book Seven)
Sophie Tracks a Thief (Book Eight)
Sophie Flakes Out (Book Nine)
Sophie Loves Jimmy (Book Ten)
Sophie Loses the Lead (Book Eleven)
Sophie's Encore (Book Twelve)

Nonfiction

No Boys Allowed: Devotions for Girls
Girlz Rock: Devotions for You
Chick Chat: More Devotions for Girls
Shine On, Girl! Devotions to Keep You Sparkling

Check out www.faithgirlz.com

faiThGirLz!

storm warning

DANDI DALEY MACKALL

ZONDERVAN.com/
AUTHORTRACKER
follow your favorite authors

Storm Warning
Copyright © 2007 by Dandi Daley Mackall
Illustrations © 2007 by Zondervan

This is a work of fiction. The characters, incidents, and dialogue are products of the author's imagi-nation and are not to be construed as real. Any resemblance to actual events or persons, living or dead, is entirely coincidental.

Requests for information should be addressed to:
Zonderkidz, *Grand Rapids, Michigan 49530*

Library of Congress Cataloging-in-Publication Data

Mackall, Dandi Daley.
Storm warning / by Dandi Daley Mackall.
    p. cm. -- (Blog on series ; [bk. 8]) (Faithgirlz!)
    Summary: In an attempt to make her father proud and bring him out of his depression, Storm joins Big Lake high school's Quiz Bowl team, but although the captain and other team members seem determined to make her fail, she has friends, family, and perhaps even God on her side.
    ISBN-13: 978-0-310-71266-4 (softcover)
    ISBN-10: 0-310-71266-1 (softcover)
    [1. High schools--Fiction. 2. Schools--Fiction. 3. Interpersonal relations--Fiction. 4. Questions and answers--Fiction. 5. Contests--Fiction. 6. Depression, Mental--Fiction. 7. Fathers and daugh-ters--Fiction. 8. Christian life--Fiction.] I. Title.
    PZ7.M1905 Sto 2007
    [Fic]--dc22

                                                                2007017875

Zonderkidz is a trademark of Zondervan.

Art direction: Laura Maitner-Mason
Illustrator: Julie Speer
Cover design: Karen Phillips
Interior design: Pamela J.L. Eicher

Illustrations used in this book were created in Adobe Illustrator.
The body text for this book is set in Cochin Medium.

Printed in the United States of America

07 08 09 10 11 • 11 10 9 8 7 6 5 4 3 2 1

So we fix our eyes not on what is seen, but on what is unseen. For what is seen is temporary, but what is unseen is eternal.

— *2 Corinthians 4:18*

1

I forgot!

Storm Novelo bolted straight up in bed. Her thoughts were spinning too fast for her to grab onto them. She'd forgotten *something*. She was sure of that.

She struggled to line up the facts. Storm was all about facts. For example, today was the day after Memorial Day. *Fact*: Memorial Day was first called Decoration Day. *Fact*: Since World War I, it has also been called Poppy Day.

No help there.

Storm shoved her long, straight black hair out of her face and squinted at the morning light peeking through her window. What was she forgetting? Homework? Only nine school days left in the year. Nine more days as a freshman at Big Lake High School. Four of the days were makeups because Big Lake, Ohio, had used up all its snow days by early January.

But Storm would never feel this kind of panic over homework. She yawned. If she could just go back to sleep ...

No way. Storm couldn't shake the feeling that she'd forgotten something major. It was more than a feeling. Close to a fact. A subconscious fact. Hadn't she just read last week that most memory lies in the subconscious? It was a great article too. About how seven items can pass through the gate of a person's short-term memory, but if you add the eighth, it's too much. And how even for seven items, the subconscious stores them better with a system, like memory hooks or mnemonics. Like remembering the colors in the rainbow as "Roy G. Biv," for red, orange, yellow, green, blue, indigo, violet.

This was so not helping.

What had she forgotten?

Her blog? Storm was part of a blogging team made up of her best friends. They worked together on a website called *That's What You Think!* She'd promised Gracie, their chief blogger, that she'd have her trivia column written by this afternoon's blog meeting. She didn't have it yet, but she would. Trivia came easily to Storm Novelo. So that wasn't it.

Then she got it. "The Mexican hat plant!"

Bounding out of bed, she raced for the door. Her shin slammed into her mother's sewing machine. "Ow!"

She pressed on, shoving aside the maze of clothes hanging like drapes all around the tiny room. Storm's bedroom served as her mother's sewing room. Since Mom had taken the customer-service job at the supermarket, the turnaround on mending jobs had gotten longer. More and more clothes kept piling up.

Storm flung open the bedroom door and dashed to the kitchen.

Her mother set down the teakettle. "Storm? What's the matter?"

"I forgot!" Storm cried, crossing the kitchen for the little makeshift greenhouse. "Dad's plant! I forgot to bring it in last night."

"Oh, Storm." Her mother didn't need to say more. Her tone said it all. Storm's father did not need this.

Bringing in that plant was the only thing Dad had asked her to do for him. He'd babied his Mexican hat plant for months. That plant was just about the only thing he'd shown interest in for weeks. He'd carried the planter from the yard to the greenhouse and back again dozens of times, depending on the forecast.

But Memorial Day was his busiest day of the whole year, the day he had to make sure the cemetery lawns stayed groomed and clean. So he'd asked Storm to see to his plant. When he'd left for the cemetery, he'd reminded her to bring in the hat plant because the forecast called for severe thunderstorms, possibly mixed with hail. For once, the weathermen had gotten it right.

Storm and her blogging buddies had spent the evening eating ice cream at Sam's Sammich Shop, the local hangout owned by Samantha Lind. Annie Lind, Sam's daughter, had driven everybody home when it started to sprinkle. Storm had been dropped off last, and the sky had opened just as she stepped out of Annie's car. She'd had to run through giant raindrops mixed with tiny ice pellets.

And still she'd forgotten all about Dad's plant.

Storm slid on the waxed kitchen linoleum as she made the turn into the tiny greenhouse. It smelled like a jungle — musty, but fresh. Her dad had built it himself out of plastic and used lumber. The greenhouse opened onto their small backyard.

There in the corner of the yard stood Storm's dad, his back toward her. He was leaning over what was left of his favorite plant.

Dear God, Storm prayed, wishing she'd thought to pray sooner, *please make Dad's plant be okay. Make* me *be okay too, while you're at it.* Storm was still new at being a Christian, and she didn't think she was a very good one yet. If she had been, she wouldn't have forgotten something that meant so much to her dad, especially when he was like this.

Storm hadn't seen her dad this depressed since they'd made the move to Ohio. As far as she could tell, the depression had crept up on him, beginning a few weeks ago and gripping him tighter every day.

And now she'd done this, making everything worse.

Mud squished through her toes as she made her way to the back of the yard. Her dad didn't turn around. He showed no sign of knowing she was there. Instead, Eduardo Novelo stared into the white planter, his back bent sideways at exactly the same angle as the scraggly plant, as if the night's storm had been too much for both of them.

"Dad, I'm so sorry."

He didn't move. He didn't look at her.

"I didn't mean to leave it outside. I got back late. And I just forgot." Her excuse sounded lame, even to her. "I should have brought it in before I went out." She wanted him to turn around, to yell at her. Shout. Scream. Anything would be better than this silence.

"Dad?" She took another step closer. "Will you forgive me? Can I do something to make it up to you? I'll work extra hours at the supermarket, okay? I can earn enough money to buy another plant just like this one." She tried to remember what he'd said about the plant. He called it a Mexican hat plant, but it had other names, like mother of thousands, and a

longer name she couldn't remember. She thought he'd ordered
it from somewhere down South.

Without looking at her, he said, "It is my fault. I was a fool
to try."

"To try what? To try to grow it here?" Storm asked.
Sometimes she had to answer her own questions when he was
like this. "Why? Because it's too cold in Ohio? Too wet?"

It was a long time before he spoke. Storm waited because
she didn't know what else to do. "In Texas," he began, his
voice barely above a whisper, "it grows like a cactus flower. I
just thought ..."

"You thought you could grow it in the greenhouse," Storm
said, finishing his sentence because he didn't seem to have the
strength to finish it himself.

"In Florida," he continued, "it grows so freely that some
think it is a weed."

Storm knew that even if everybody else in the whole
world considered that plant a weed, her dad didn't. He called
dandelions flowers. If dandelions didn't grow so easily, he
insisted, they would be considered rare and beautiful flowers.
Although he pulled them out of other people's yards, he took
great care to grow them in his own yard. He'd cultivated
dandelions to frame their whole backyard. She glanced
around at the dandelions and was surprised to see how
overgrown everything looked.

"It doesn't matter," he said, finally.

But it did matter. Storm knew it did, as much as anything
could matter to her dad now. What she didn't understand was
why it mattered so much. "Is the flower from Mexico?" she
asked. There had been two blooms on the plant before the

storm, and they really did look like Mexican hats, with tall centers and low petals that made the brim of a hat.

Her father shook his head. Storm caught a glimpse of his face, wrinkled and brown from hours in the sun doing yard work for rich people. "The flower comes from Madagascar," he said softly.

"But your parents grew them when you were a boy, right?" She was in dangerous territory now. She could almost see her dad growing smaller, sinking into himself. Her dad's mother had died before Storm was born. His father, Storm's only living grandparent, had never visited them. And they had never gone to Chicago to see him, at least not that Storm remembered. He'd remarried and had a whole new family now.

"I should have kept the plant in the greenhouse," her dad said. He'd turned his back on Storm again, so it sounded like he was talking to the leafless stalk of a plant. "I just wanted it to see the sun."

"'Time for breakfast!" Storm's mother called from the kitchen, her voice loud and clear through the kitchen window.

Storm waited for her dad, but he didn't seem to hear. Usually, whenever Storm's mother called, her dad hopped to it. Tina Novelo was small, like Storm, not much over five feet and not a pound over one hundred. But she had an air of authority and strength about her. Storm's dad called her his Mayan princess.

Storm touched her dad's arm. "Dad? We better — "

"Storm, you'll be late for school!" her mother shouted.

Storm started to say something to her dad, then gave up and walked inside. She wasn't hungry, but she sat at the kitchen table anyway. "Won't Dad even come in for breakfast?" she asked.

Her mother poured hot water into an old teacup, the cream paint cracked and stained. "Your father isn't hungry."

Storm hadn't seen her dad eat in three days, but she didn't question her mom. Her parents knew each other too well. They'd had a secret language her whole life, a way of communicating without words. Her mom knew her dad better than Storm would ever know either one of them.

"Why is he acting like this?" Storm asked, sipping the orange juice set on the table for her. There were three glasses of juice set out. A full Spanish omelet sat waiting in the pan on the stove. Maybe Tina Novelo didn't know her husband as well as she thought she did.

"Your father is depressed. You know that."

"But why? I don't know why."

Her mother sat down at the small kitchen table. "There's not always a *why* to know."

Storm waited for more, but she didn't get it. Finally, she went to her room and got dressed for school. She chose bright yellow — a yellow peasant blouse and a yellow peasant skirt. She reached for her yellow flowered sandals, the ones she'd bought at a garage sale for a dollar. Then she thought better of it. Why wear a built-in reminder of the flower disaster?

Storm studied herself in the mirror as she swept up her straight hair into a ponytail. She'd hoped bright yellow would change her mood. But so far, it wasn't working. She couldn't get the picture out of her head, the image of her dad slumping like the wind-broken stem.

2

Back in the kitchen, Storm sat at the table to wait for her ride to school, while her mom sloshed water in the sink to get it to drain. "Do you think it's my fault?" Storm asked.

"Why? Did you put something down the drain you shouldn't have?" Mom snapped.

"Not that," Storm said. "Dad. Is he depressed because of me?" She knew she did a dozen careless things every day. She forgot to close drawers, or clean sinks, or put dishes away. And she could be harsh in what she said too, speaking without thinking. Since she'd become a Christian, it seemed like she'd gotten worse, instead of better.

"No," her mother answered. "It's not your fault."

"Is it because of Memorial Day? Does he miss his mother? Maybe we should call my grandfather. We could invite him to come and visit."

Storm's mom took in a deep breath and walked over to the stove. "I believe he does think of his mother — and his father — especially around Memorial Day." She slid the uneaten omelet onto a plate and took out the cellophane wrap. "But I'm not sure he misses them. Not in the way you're thinking."

"He doesn't miss them? Were they mean to him?" Storm had always wanted to know about her grandparents, but neither her mother or father ever wanted to talk about them.

"Your father's parents were good people," her mother said, "but hard."

"Hard? How?" Storm had a million questions. She waited, hoping this wasn't all she would get. "Why don't Dad and my grandfather talk to each other? It doesn't make sense."

"We've tried. Your father has tried. It's caused him a great deal of pain. To your grandparents, Eddy was a disappointment. Now, when he sees himself through their eyes — when he remembers, as he does on Memorial Day — your father feels like a failure."

"But he's not!" Storm protested. "He works so hard. And he has his own business. He should feel proud." Storm felt a pang of guilt. It hadn't been that long ago when she wasn't exactly proud of her dad. She'd tried to keep her friends from meeting her parents. It had been pretty bent. Storm never had as much money as her friends. She was always cashed out when they wanted to go to a movie or something. There'd been a time when she hadn't wanted anybody to see the little house her parents rented. She'd tried to keep her social life far away from her home life.

But she'd changed. Her parents may not have owned their own home or driven a nice car, but they were good people and good parents. Her dad worked hard to support his family. He had his own truck, ran his own lawn-care business. She was proud of him. She hoped he knew that.

"Your father's and grandfather's problems are old, Storm." Mom sounded tired.

"Tell me," Storm begged.

Her mother appeared to be thinking it over. Then she took the chair across the table from Storm. "I don't ever want you to bring this up again. Is that understood?"

Storm nodded.

Her mother glanced toward the door, probably making sure Dad wasn't there. "Your father went to high school in Chicago. He did well enough in school, though it wasn't easy for him. His parents set their hopes on having him earn a scholarship and be the first in his family to attend college.

"When the neighbor's son, who was two years older than Eduardo, won a scholarship playing football, Eddy's parents insisted he play football too. He was good enough to make the team — fast and smart — but he loved soccer, a sport his father hated. Your grandfather thought soccer was 'Old World,' and he wanted his son to be 'All-American,' like the neighbors' sons. These other boys in the old neighborhood brought home letters for their fathers, letters which were proudly displayed, letters that opened doors for scholarships to colleges. There were no letters in soccer."

"Letters? Like varsity letters?"

Her mom nodded. "Mr. Novelo believed a school letter stood as a symbol of all-American success."

"You're kidding," Storm said. She'd always found that kind of rah-rah stuff pretty lame.

Her mom shook her head. "Your father's parents watched their friends' children earn these magical letters. One in basketball. Another in football. And your father came home empty-handed. Their friends' children went off to colleges and universities. Your father took a job mowing lawns. The distance between them grew. Then your father and I married and moved away from Chicago."

It was the most information Storm had ever been given about her parents' lives before she was born. She wasn't sure what to do with it. "And you really think that's why Dad is so depressed?"

"I told you, Storm. There's not a good reason why your father goes through these times of depression. It's not that easy. He has seen a doctor, but we can't afford for him to go often."

Storm wouldn't let it go. "But you think he's thinking about it, don't you? About not getting that stupid letter for his parents? About being a failure to them?"

Her mother shrugged. She got up from the table and poured her tea down the sink. The conversation was obviously over, as far as she was concerned.

A horn honked outside. Storm slung her book-heavy backpack over one shoulder and headed for the door. Then she turned back. "Is there anything I can do to make Dad better?"

The little laugh her mother let out sounded bitter. It wasn't like her stoic mother to be bitter, or to show it at least. "Can you turn back time?" she asked evenly. "Can you bring your father a varsity letter?"

Storm didn't answer. She'd never played a sport and had no desire to start now.

"No," said her mother. "I didn't think so."

The car radio was blaring so loud that Storm heard it as soon as she stepped outside. Annie waved, never stopping her bobbing and weaving to the beat.

Automatically, Storm began to roll up her skirt at the waist. But as she reached for the car door, she realized what she was doing.

Before she'd come to know Christ, Storm had left the house in one outfit and changed into other threads before she got to school. It hadn't bothered her a bit to deceive her parents like that. She hadn't even considered it deception. What they didn't know couldn't hurt them, she'd reasoned. And her short skirts and tight tanks weren't really hurting anybody else either.

But she'd stopped doing that. It *was* deception, no matter how she'd rationalized it. She could see that now. Yet here she was, hiking up her peasant skirt as soon as she was out of her mom's sight. She yanked it back where it belonged and hopped into the passenger's seat, wondering if she'd ever really change.

"Hey, Storm! Nice outfit. Sweet! Very yellow. Very you." Annie Lind was wearing her cheerleading outfit. With her perfect auburn hair, big blue eyes, and even bigger smile, Annie was undoubtedly the most popular sophomore at Big Lake High School. You couldn't *not* like Annie. She was a head taller than Storm, so Storm looked up to her in more ways than one.

Even though Storm was just a freshman, she had a couple of sophomore classes with Annie because she'd tested out of her freshman history and English. She took science with juniors.

Storm didn't believe she was all that smart — not like Cameron, the graduating senior everybody knew would be valedictorian. Or Lane, a junior in Storm's science class. Cameron and Lane were on the Quiz Bowl. They even looked smart. Storm, on the other hand, knew she looked anything but smart, which was the way she liked it, to tell the truth. She just read a lot. And she remembered what she read.

"Thanks for coming by for me," Storm said, buckling her seatbelt. The car, which belonged to Annie's mother, smelled like vanilla, thanks to the scented ball dangling from the rearview mirror.

Annie cleared her throat. The car hadn't moved. Storm stared out the window at the rental house, which could have used a fresh coat of paint. She was glad she couldn't see her backyard. Or her dad.

"Well?" Annie sounded impatient.

Storm turned to see why. "Well what?"

Annie sighed. "Storm! Don't you notice anything different?" Annie bounced in the driver's seat, making Storm remember the first time she'd figured out who Annie was.

Before moving to Big Lake, Storm had read blogs. Her favorite online blog had been *That's What You Think!*, where someone calling herself "Jane" wrote about "Typical High" and the kids who went there, including "Bouncy Perky Girl." Once Storm enrolled at Big Lake, it had only taken her a couple of days to figure out that the school she'd been reading about was in reality her new school, Big Lake High School, and "Bouncy Perky Girl" was none other than Annie Lind. Storm's discoveries about the anonymous website had stirred up a lot of trouble in the beginning. But in the end, they'd formed a blogging team together. Annie and the others on the blog team were the best friends Storm had ever had.

Annie bounced again. "Hello? Look at me, Storm! Don't you notice anything different about me today?"

"You're bouncier than usual?" Storm tried.

"You are so dense." Annie turned her back on Storm. "*Now* do you see it?"

"New jacket?" Storm guessed. She figured she was probably right, since it was too warm to wear a jacket for any reason except that it was new.

"Duh, yeah!" Annie exclaimed, still keeping her back to Storm.

Then Storm saw it. "It's a letter jacket." How weird was that? She could have gone her whole life without thinking about letter jackets. But here was Annie, jazzed up about this stupid letter, a letter Storm's grandparents had wanted so much for their son. Sometimes life made absolutely no sense.

Annie shifted in her seat and put the car into gear before pulling away from the curb.

Storm leaned around to get a better look. A big letter "L" had been sewn onto the back of the jacket. "Why *L*?" she asked.

"What else would it be, Storm? You only get one letter. The school couldn't give out Bs for *Big* Lake. That would be too ditzoid. I guess they could have used *S* for Sharks, but that would be bent, if you ask me. Big Lake High has always been *L*. Haven't you ever seen a letter jacket before?"

Storm shrugged. She probably had. She just hadn't paid attention. "Maybe I saw Bryce and Jared wearing jackets like that. Guess I just assumed the *L* stood for *Loser*," she teased.

"Funny," Annie replied, not laughing.

"So whose jacket is it?" If Storm hadn't lost track, Annie's latest guy was Casey. Or maybe Stan again? Annie went out with a lot of guys, which was why her blog was called "Professor Love." She gave advice to the lovelorn.

"The jacket's mine!" Annie answered. "As in, my own letter jacket and not just something loaned to me by one of the guys."

"Seriously, Annie, where did you get it?" Storm knew Annie was no more an athlete than she was. Mick, the webmaster for their blog site, was the baseball player. She'd probably earn a bunch of letters when she got to high school.

"It *is* mine!" Annie insisted. "For cheering! We did competition this year too. Remember? High school letters don't just go to jocks anymore, Storm. Where've you been? You can letter in band, music, all kinds of activities. I earned this letter fair and square. And it means a lot to me, so don't mock me out. Okay?"

Annie was right. Storm should have known the school letter would mean something major to her friend. Once again, Storm wondered how long it would take for her to become a better person, a good Christian. "I'm sorry, Annie."

They were quiet for a minute. Storm knew Annie couldn't stay mad at anybody. Sometimes she wished she could be more like her friend. Annie got sentimental over lots of things Storm found silly. "Annie," she began, "tell me what it means. The jacket. The letter. Why is it such a big deal to you?"

Annie glanced at her, as if checking to see whether or not Storm was really asking or just making fun. "Seriously?"

"Seriously. I need to know. Why is that letter so important?"

"It means I belong," Annie explained. "I fit. I'm one of the guys. The girls. You know? I mattered on a team. Twenty years from now, I'll be able to look at this letter and know that I was really a part of my high school."

Maybe that was it. Maybe that was why a stupid letter had meant so much to her grandparents. They'd been trying desperately to fit in, and they wanted their son to be part of this new life in a new country. Was that how her dad felt too? Did he still feel like he didn't belong, that he'd never fit? Did he worry about *her*? Was he afraid she wouldn't fit either?

"My dad always wanted to letter in something," Storm said. "His parents wanted it even more than he did. It ruined their relationship when he was in high school." Even a month ago, Storm wouldn't have admitted such a thing to anybody. She would have kept on pretending that things were fine at home, that her life was perfect and carefree.

Storm had already confided to Annie that her dad was suffering from depression. Now she told her friend as much as she knew about why.

"I'm sorry, Storm," Annie said when Storm had finished relaying her conversation with her mother that morning. They were in the parking lot, the car turned off. "I never should have gone on and on about my stupid letter."

"I'm glad you did." Storm meant it too. "At least it all makes a little more sense now." Not that it helped her dad any. "Hey," Storm said, trying to lighten things up again. "Don't suppose your cheerleading squad could use another cheerleader, huh?"

Annie laughed. "You?"

They both knew how Storm felt about cheering. Or as Storm like to put it, "jumping up and down in an outfit shared by seven other girls."

"You think I can't be a cheerleader?" Storm asked, trying not to laugh. She bounded out of the car, twirled three times in a fake ballerina move, then leaped as high as she could. "See? Go, go, Sharks! I love parks!" She kept twirling and jumping higher and higher. "Love my school! I'm so cool!"

"Storm, look out!" Annie cried.

But it was too late. Storm was in midair. She came down hard, crashing into somebody with all one hundred pounds of force. Down they tumbled to the sidewalk.

Storm had a soft landing, thanks to the fact that she landed on top. "Sorry!" She scurried off and backed away. Only then did she see the guy she'd knocked over. Cameron — Quiz-Bowl Captain, Mr. Valedictorian — Worthington the Third.

"Cameron? Are you okay?" she shouted down.

He lay on the ground, the wind obviously knocked out of him. It was probably the only thing keeping him from screaming at her, as his mouth moved soundlessly.

"I'm so sorry!" Storm exclaimed. But the sight of the tall, austere senior silently cursing her, growing more frustrated as words failed him, made her laugh. "My bad," she said, reaching down to give him a hand.

He brushed her away, refusing her help. The motion was so awkward and anger-filled, it made her laugh even more. She couldn't help herself.

In the year's final issue of the school newspaper, Cameron Worthington the Third had been voted Least Likely to Laugh.

He was living up to his reputation.

3

Storm and Annie stood around until they were sure Cameron was okay. He lay on the sidewalk for a minute. But when the bell rang, he sprang to his feet.

"Was that the last bell?" he asked, sounding horrified.

"Uh-huh," Annie answered, keeping a safe distance from him.

"I can't believe this," he muttered, brushing off his brown slacks. He was cute. Nice build. Great hair. Intense brown eyes. But Storm couldn't remember ever seeing him smile.

She gathered the books and papers he'd dropped, chasing down a couple of pieces of notebook paper. "I think I got everything," she said, handing him the stack.

Cameron grabbed the books and clutched them to his chest as if Storm had tried to steal them from him. "Two weeks from the end of my senior year in high school, and I'm late to class. I've never been late to class, not once in my whole school career! Not even when my dad's car broke down in sixth grade and I had to run the rest of the way to school."

Storm thought he was talking to himself until he glared down at her. "And now *you* run over me and make me late!"

Storm tried not to grin. But she was half his size, if that. "Sorry?" she tried.

"Well, that's for certain. You are definitely *sorry!*" And with that, Cameron Worthington the Third stormed into the school building at top speed.

Storm felt bad now. The guy was right. She *was* pretty sorry. A sorry excuse for a Christian anyway. Wasn't she supposed to be a better person now? Instead, what had she done? Knocked Cameron down to the ground. True, that part wasn't on purpose. But she'd laughed at him while he was down.

God, she prayed, as she followed Annie inside, *I just hope you're not sorry you took me on. I sure have a long way to go.*

Storm had art first hour. Ms. B, their teacher, was so busy setting up yet another still life for them to draw, that she didn't seem to notice when Storm walked in late. Storm moved to the back row and slid into the seat between Gracie and Jazz, two of her fellow blog-team members.

"Nice you could make it, Storm," Jazz whispered. Jazz was the one with the talent. She could draw or paint anything. Storm fully expected her to be a famous artist one day. Jazz did cartoons for *That's What You Think!* and graphics for the whole site.

"You missed me!" Storm replied, dabbing at the corner of her eye, as if tearing up. "I had no idea you cared so much, Jazz."

Jazz merely raised her eyebrows. She and Storm were the freshmen on the blog team, and Storm loved Jazz's dry sense of humor. Made her fun to joke with.

Gracie leaned in and asked, "Are you finished yet?" Grace Doe did not waste words. At least she didn't waste them on speech. She *wrote* words all the time, blogging more than the rest of them put together. Gracie had started *That's What You*

Think! all by herself. Now, she functioned as their unofficial captain, keeping everybody on track. Or at least, trying to.

"Finished?" Storm repeated, pulling out her most puzzled look. "As in finished talking to Jazz? Or finished doing this still life? Because I haven't even started the still life yet." Storm knew Gracie was asking if she'd finished her trivia blog yet. Storm called her blog "Didyanose" because she usually started it with "Did you know . . . ?" But it was fun to tease Gracie because she was so serious about her website.

Gracie, however, didn't take the bait. "Have it by our blog meeting, Storm. Four thirty. The cottage."

"Fasheezy, Captain!" Storm promised. She pulled out her notebook and tried to remember the blog theme for this week. She started to ask Gracie, but Gracie had already begun to sketch and didn't look like she wanted to be disturbed.

Storm turned to ask Jazz, but Jazz had moved to an empty seat next to the window. Storm knew Jazz hated drawing stills. She'd probably work on a landscape, something she'd spotted out the window. Or maybe she'd create one of her abstracts.

Since Storm couldn't remember this week's blog theme, she decided to make up her own. Her favorite trivia was food trivia, so that's what she'd write about. Hopefully, when she did find out the blog theme, she could come up with a creative way to tie her blog into everyone else's. She'd pulled it off before.

For now, she'd just jot down whatever popped into her mind:

Did you know . . . ?

Pound cake got its name because the recipe called for a whole pound of butter.

Donuts were invented in 1847 by a 15-year-old baker's apprentice, who knocked the center out of some fried dough and liked the way it looked.

Pepper used to be the most expensive seasoning in the world.

In Japan, the bestselling baby food is sardines.

The biggest menu item in the world is roast camel, usually stuffed with a sheep, which is stuffed with chickens, which are stuffed with fish, which are stuffed with eggs ... Enough said?

The Food and Drug Administration guidelines tell us what can and what can't be in peanut butter. It says it's okay if 30 insect fragments and one or two rodent hairs show up per 100 grams of peanut butter. May be okay with them (and I'll bet they don't eat peanut butter), but it's so NOT okay with me!

The fact about pepper didn't really fit, so she crossed it out. Storm didn't really believe the one about peanut butter. She'd read the stat on the Internet, and you couldn't always trust what you found there. She preferred books. All kinds of books. Someday Storm intended to have her own set of encyclopedias. Her own library even.

"Storm? Storm?" Ms. B said it loud enough to get Storm's attention.

Storm looked up from her notes, surprised to see Ms. B, and just about everybody else in class, staring at her. "Yes, Ms. Biederman?"

"I hope you're coming along on your still life, Storm, and not working on homework for some other class." Ms. Biederman folded her arms in front of her without wrinkling her perfectly pressed beige blouse.

"Homework? No way!" Storm did put away the notebook, though, and started trying to draw the vase of flowers sitting on Ms. B's desk. "Thanks for the heads-up, Gracie," Storm whispered.

Storm thought she detected a grin playing on Gracie's lips. "Hey, who am I to tell you to stop working on your blog?"

Storm felt a tinge of guilt. Ms. B had always been pretty decent to her. Even though Storm didn't have a bit of talent or artistic ability, their art teacher seemed to think she did. And still, Storm spent about half of each art class doing other things. *One more thing wrong with me,* Storm thought. Unbelievable.

Storm's science class this semester focused on genetics. The class consisted of twenty juniors, two seniors, and one freshman — Storm. One of the seniors, Cameron, was taking the class as an elective because his science classes hadn't covered genetics extensively. Storm wondered what his other electives were. Physics? Advanced trig?

Mr. Hammer talked in a monotone, as if every word had the same importance. Storm could imagine him announcing "Class, the school is on fire, and we will all burn to charcoal" with the exact same inflection as he announced "Class, we will pair up for this next science experiment," which was what he did announce about halfway through the hour.

Mr. Hammer paired them off scientifically, pointing down each row and saying, "You and you. You and you. You and you." Cameron always sat in the first row, the last seat on the left. Usually, this paired him with Aaron Baxter, quite possibly the only person in class Cameron considered smart enough to be his partner. They were on Quiz Bowl together.

But this time, Aaron wasn't there. That meant Cameron's partner would fall to the first person in the next row. Storm.

"... And you," Mr. Hammer said, moving all the way to the other side of the room to point at Storm.

"No!" Cameron objected.

"Excuse me?" Mr. Hammer said.

"Aaron and I are partners," Cameron said. "We're always lab partners."

"Aaron's not here," Mr. Hammer pointed out.

Cameron glanced over at Storm, as if he expected her to pounce on him again.

She grinned and waved. Poor Cameron.

"But where is Aaron?" Cameron demanded. "Is he sick?"

Mr. Hammer frowned. "I thought you knew, Cameron. Aren't you boys friends?"

"Knew what?" Cameron asked, not exactly answering the "friend" question.

"Aaron moved away. He took his finals early. It was all arranged through the office. It seems his whole family is making the move to California."

"He can't be gone!" Cameron insisted.

"I'm sure you and Miss Novelo will get along just fine," Mr. Hammer reassured him.

"Because I love to experiment and blow up stuff!" Storm exclaimed.

Even Mr. Hammer laughed. Everyone did, except Cameron.

The experiment was pretty straightforward, probably because the year was almost out and Mr. Hammer didn't want to risk wrecking anything at this late date. Each team was given supplies to simulate the canning process.

"What does this have to do with genetics?" Cameron asked.

Storm had to admit he did have a point.

"Nothing directly," Mr. Hammer admitted. "I just thought it might be fun."

Wrong answer. Storm could see the strands in Cameron's neck twist.

"Your task," Mr. Hammer explained, "is to seal your containers without leaving any air inside."

Cameron took charge, as if Storm didn't even exist.

She moved into Aaron's old spot and scooted her chair next to his. "How's tricks, Cameron?" she asked.

He didn't even glance over at her.

She watched as he bent the piece of tin into a lid for their can. "So," she tried, "you feeling all right?" It occurred to her at that moment that what they were supposed to do was exactly what had happened to Cameron outside. "Wow! Cameron, all we need to do is knock the air out! You know? Just like you got the wind knocked out of you!"

He shot her an angry look.

She worked it all out in her head. It really would work. "Seriously, Cameron. I'm not kidding around."

"Right." He took the paper wrappers off the two straws provided in their experiment packet.

Storm glanced around the room and saw that most of the lab teams were trying the same thing Cameron was. They thought they could suck out the air. Couldn't they see that it wouldn't work? She strongly suspected that Mr. Hammer had tossed in the straws to throw them off track. She was positive her idea would work — sudden impact, knocking the air out.

"Cameron, if you — " Storm started to explain why the straw routine was bound to fail, but she could see he'd never listen. Some people were like that.

For the rest of the class period, she sat back and let Cameron do his thing without her.

"Time's up!" Mr. Hammer announced.

Cameron shoved his unfinished can to the edge of his desk. Groans sounded around the classroom.

"I have to say I'm rather disappointed," Mr. Hammer confided. "None of you have been successful. Just because you have access to straws doesn't mean the solution lies in those straws. Think outside the box. If we were canning vegetables, you would have failed. Your vegetables would rot before they reached consumer shelves. So what can we learn from this?" He paused. "What do you have to say, class?"

Nobody said anything.

"Anybody?" Mr. Hammer urged. "Cameron? Someone?"

"Did you know the first vegetable to be canned commercially was the carrot?" Storm asked. "Seems like a waste to me, but there you have it."

"I did not know that," Mr. Hammer admitted.

"People used to grow carrots for medicine instead of food," Storm went on. "Now *that,* I believe. I've always thought carrots tasted more like medicine than food."

"That's very interesting," Mr. Hammer said.

"Lots of people are supposedly allergic to them. To carrots, I mean," Storm continued. "I always thought Mel Blanc was allergic to carrots, which was kind of funny since he was the voice of Bugs Bunny — you know, the 'What's-up-Doc?' guy.

Turns out he wasn't though. Wasn't allergic. He just didn't like carrots."

"Very enlightening. Well done, Miss Novelo," Mr. Hammer said, smiling. "Perhaps we've all learned something today after all."

Cameron frowned over at her. If looks could kill, she'd be history.

4

Storm joined Annie at the cheerleaders' table for lunch. She'd forgotten to pack her lunch, and she didn't have cash for school lunch. But she wasn't that hungry anyway.

Annie tossed her a bag of chips from her tray. "Why would they give these chips out with a tuna sandwich?" she asked. "Like I need potato chips? I've got to lose a couple pounds to fit into last-year's swimsuit. Storm, *please* eat my potato chips!"

Storm couldn't imagine where two pounds would come from with Annie. She was so not overweight and probably never would be, if she had her mother's genes. Samantha Lind still had her high-school figure. Storm ripped open the bag and started in on all seven chips vacuum packed inside.

Bridget Crawford, a sophomore who was almost as bouncy and perky as Annie, leaned over and appeared to study the back of Annie's jacket. "I think you put the letter too low, Annie." Bridget swept her long bleached-blonde hair to the front of one shoulder and swiveled around so everyone could check out *her* varsity letter. "I put mine exactly where the regulation book said to."

Annie craned her neck, trying to see her non-regulation letter. "Really? Do you think it's too low?"

Storm could read Bridget like a bad novel. The girl just wanted to make sure everyone noticed *her* letter, even if it meant making Annie feel bad. Storm couldn't sit by and see her friend upset for no good reason. "Actually, Annie, your letter is perfect. We can see it." She turned to Bridget. "I honestly didn't notice your letter, Bridget. Your hair covers it. Guess you'll have to get a haircut if you want anybody to see your *L*."

"She's right, Bridget," Sasha said. She was one of the nicest cheerleaders, not counting Annie.

The rest of lunch, Bridget spent fidgeting with her letter, or pulling her hair to the front.

Most of the table conversation centered around who had gotten letters and who hadn't. Storm hadn't bothered attending the awards' assembly Sunday night because she wasn't getting one. She tried to tune out the varsity-letter discussion. It kept bringing her back to her dad and his depression, which made her feel depressed.

Tuning out Bridget's monologue about all the cheerleaders in her family's history, Storm tuned in to the conversation going on at the table behind her. She recognized Cameron's voice, but had to turn around to see who he was talking to. It was Lane Busan, a sophomore Korean-American student, whose family must have lived in America for generations. Lane and Cameron leaned across the table so their heads were just inches apart. In spite of the body language, Storm didn't think they were going out or talking or anything. She scooted over where she could hear them better.

"What's the only man-made object visible from space?" Lane asked.

"The Great Wall of China," Cameron answered. "Too easy. Go to the questions in the back of the book."

Storm wasn't sure what they were doing, but she couldn't keep quiet. She turned around. "Hey, guys! Couldn't help overhearing. You know? About the Great Wall of China being the only man-made object visible from space?"

Cameron squinted over at her like *she'd* come from space. She pressed on. "Actually, if you're close enough to see a thin ribbon of stone, you could see a lot of other objects."

"No you can't." Lane tapped her big black book with her index finger. "It says so right here."

Storm shrugged. "On the Gemini Five flight, they could see Launch Complex Thirty-Nine, the one used for Apollo missions. Some people reported that Cooper and Conrad said they could see a checkerboard pattern laid out in Texas too. There's this great picture of the Nile Delta from a hundred miles up in space, and you can see lines of river highways that — "

"If you don't mind," Cameron said firmly, "we're working here."

Storm turned back to the cheerleader table, but she'd lost her appetite, even for the remaining three chips in the bag.

It was turning into the longest lunch period on record. Now that Storm was forced to listen to the varsity-letter conversations again, she couldn't keep her mind from sliding back to her dad. She could still see him slumped over the ruined plant.

Without thinking about it, she ate another potato chip. *Rats!* She'd forgotten to say grace. Again. True, it was just a few chips. And there wasn't a Bible law about saying grace before meals. But Storm had promised herself she'd do it. She wanted to thank God more. And she wanted to remember to pray more.

On her way out of the cafeteria, Storm caught up with Gracie. Gracie always refused to eat at the cheerleading table because she claimed too much bounciness made her nauseated. "What's up, Gracie girl?" Storm shouted.

Gracie gave her a grin. Storm thought, not for the first time, that Grace Doe was extremely pretty, in spite of herself. Gracie's preferred school uniform was black. Black pants. Black T-shirt. Maybe an army jacket thrown in. She wore her hair short and straight and never bothered with makeup. But she had a natural beauty that radiated, even when she went around frowning and scribbling in her notebook, making her observations about other people's lives. Gracie could be serious, even too serious, but she was a loyal friend. And she'd had a lot to do with Storm's decision to become a Christian.

Gracie didn't slow down when she hit the crowded hall. "How's the trivia blog coming, Storm?" she called over her shoulder as Storm jogged to keep up.

"No worries," Storm promised. "Virtually finished," she lied. As soon as the words were out, Storm wanted to take them back. It was a "little" lie, but a lie. Would she ever get the hang of being a Christian?

Storm didn't get a chance to work on her trivia column until last hour. She took history with the sophomores and usually sat with Annie and Gracie somewhere toward the back. As soon as she got to class, she dug out her blog notes and went to work.

"You two are fun," Annie said sarcastically.

Gracie didn't look up from her stenographer's notebook. Storm knew Gracie must be writing down observations. She'd filled notebooks with gestures and body-language cues, and she could read people. It was pretty amazing, actually, the things Grace Doe could tell about people, simply by observing a shift of the jaw, a blink, or the position of the feet or hands when talking.

Storm was just as intent, working on her "Didyanose" column. She tried to pick up where she'd left off, but it wasn't easy. Sighing, she smiled over at Annie. "Sorry. I've got this *person* on my back, nagging me to finish my blog. You know how it is."

"I do," Annie replied, elbowing Gracie. "Which is why I've already passed Professor Love's blog to Mick the Munch."

"Such dedication," Gracie commented, without looking up from her notes. "Such discipline."

Storm knew Gracie was just kidding around. But she was right. Dedication and discipline were two qualities Storm had hoped she'd get when she'd accepted Christ. So far, they didn't seem to be part of the package.

As soon as Mr. Stovall started lecturing, Gracie switched notebooks and took notes on the lecture. Mr. Stovall was known as "Bones" in Gracie's blogs. She'd studied his gestures, and it seemed to Storm that Grace Doe knew when their teacher would give them a pop quiz, even before he knew it.

Annie wrote notes too, but a different kind of note. Hers, she passed to tall, dark, and handsome Eric, sitting next to her.

Storm took advantage of the time to continue working on her blog:

Hamburgers were invented by Louis Lassen in 1900. He had the crazy idea of grinding up beef, broiling it, and then putting it between two pieces of toast. And now hamburgers are the #2 food ordered in restaurants. What's #1? French fries!

The first cereal invented to be sold for breakfast was Shredded Wheat. It was a far cry from today's Chocolate Marshmallow Sugar-Coated Frosting-Covered Yummies, huh?

Don't get me started on potato chips! A pound of potato chips costs 200 times more than a pound of potatoes.

Storm was only half-listening to "Bones's" lecture about the aftermath of the Korean War, when she heard him say, "Class, could I please have your attention?"

Storm glanced at the clock. Ten minutes before school would be out. Now he wanted their attention?

"We have an important announcement. As some of you know, I am the sponsor for our Big Lake High School Quiz Bowl team, the BLHSQB." He glanced around the room, as if expecting applause and surprised at not getting it. "Well, I'll let one of our team members explain. You all know Lane Busan. Lane, will you come up, please?"

Lane, who always sat front-row center, stood up and turned to face the class. If she was nervous, it didn't show, at least not to Storm. "Quiz Bowl finals are a week from Saturday, and — "

"And we would care because ... ?" Bridget interrupted, ending her question with a giant yawn.

Lane frowned as if she couldn't be bothered with Bridget. "And we're short one team member since Aaron dropped out."

"Actually, Aaron and his family moved away," Mr. Stovall explained. "I'm sure he didn't mean to leave us in this undesirable position."

"Well, he did, didn't he," Lane said. "I know most of you wouldn't qualify for Quiz Bowl — "

"Thanks a lot!" somebody shouted.

Lane forged ahead. "But we're making this general announcement just the same, in case there might be somebody who at least wouldn't bring the team down."

"Like any of us would want to join the Geek Bowl," Bridget said. "I mean, the Quiz Bowl."

"We have a good time," Mr. Stovall said, his voice flat and unconvincing. "We wouldn't expect a great deal out of you, since we only have a week to work with you before out last Quiz Bowl competition."

When nobody said anything, Mr. Stovall continued, "You may have some questions. Feel free to ask Lane anything you want to know about Quiz Bowl."

Storm raised her hand. "Why is it called a bowl?"

"What?" Lane's face wrinkled up like she smelled something gross.

"Why is it Quiz *Bowl*?" Storm repeated. "Why not Quiz Contest? Or Quiz Competition? Or Trivia Quiz? On the other hand, where do we get the word *quiz*? It sounds so much more fun than it turns out to be. Who named it a Quiz Bowl?"

"How should *I* know?" Lane demanded.

Storm remembered something she'd read about the word *trivia*. "Did you know *trivia* probably comes from *tri-*, for 'three,' and *via*, for 'road'? So it was like this place where three roads met! And in Roman times, there would usually be a tavern wherever three roads came together — and not a very nice tavern at that. Not a lot of important talk going on there, if you get my drift. So whenever someone talked about things that weren't important, people started saying, 'That guy talks like he came from a tavern where three roads met.' *Trivia!* Get it?"

Lane looked away from Storm, as if Storm hadn't even spoken. "Well, is anyone interested in being on our team and competing with us?" Lane asked.

Competing? "Did you say competing?" Storm asked. "As in, *competition?* Like a sport?"

"Quiz Bowl is much harder than any sport," Lane said defensively.

The class groaned. Bridget said, "Puh-leeze!"

Storm's brain started bouncing like a bouncy perky girl. "Wait a minute! If Quiz Bowl is a competition, then the school has to give letters, right? Do people on the team get varsity letters?"

"Cameron's getting his fourth this year," Lane said, as if proving some point. "Aaron would have gotten his third, if he hadn't left us in the lurch like this."

"Actually, Lane," Mr. Stovall interrupted, "I've decided to send Aaron a letter. He did earn it this year."

Lane frowned her disapproval, but she didn't object out loud. "I got one too," she said, "even though we haven't had our last competition."

"So whoever joins your team will get a letter, right?" Storm asked, making sure.

"You have to *earn* the letter," Lane explained, as if Storm were an idiot. "There are points for making practices. Points for participating in competitions."

Storm's hope began to fade. "You don't get a letter unless you earn all these points?"

"Well," Mr. Stovall said, "final competition affords a number of required points. Plus, the awarding of the letter is up to the discretion of the sponsor. Someone who joined our Quiz Bowl in our hour of need would prove vital to the team in my estimation."

"Sweet!" Storm exclaimed. This was way too much of a coincidence not to be God. Storm's dad wanted a varsity letter, and Storm was going to get it for him. "Okay," Storm said, slapping her desk. "I'll do it!"

5

"You?" Lane wheeled on Storm. "What do you mean you'll do it?"

"The Bowl gig!" Storm exclaimed. "Quiz Bowl? The competition. Whatever it takes to get that letter ... I'll do it!"

Bridget laughed loud. "Good one, Storm! Who *wouldn't* want to join the Geek Squad, right? Guess *I* better sign up too. Do we get an *L* for *Big Lake*, or a *G* for *Geek*?"

Annie whispered to Storm, "Think about this, Storm. I know why you want to do it. But ... Quiz Bowl? There's got to be a better way."

Storm knew Annie was right. Even Bridget had a point. "Geek by association" was one of high school's unwritten laws. A month ago, Storm never would have considered joining the smart people. Her whole life, she'd done everything she could to hide her brains. When trivia or facts slipped out, she'd turn them into jokes and go for the laugh. She had successfully convinced just about everybody that she was a dark-haired version of a ditzy blonde.

Storm had been an expert in hiding her intelligence — until Grace Doe had come along. Gracie had seen through the act and figured out exactly what Storm had been doing and why.

But what about now? True, Storm wasn't crazy about being considered brainy or uncool. "Cool" had always been part of who she was. Yet, what did it matter really? Why should she care what Bridget thought about her? Or what Lane thought about her, for that matter?

Storm glanced at Gracie. She couldn't read the expression on her friend's face, but she was sure Gracie could read hers.

"Not kidding around here, guys," Storm said firmly. "I want to be on the Quiz Bowl."

The room fell silent.

Mr. Stovall jumped to action. "Terrific! Storm, that's great!"

"She *can't* join!" Lane protested. "She's a flake!"

"Is there a rule against flakes in the Bowl?" Storm asked.

Gracie laughed. So did a couple of others. Annie looked like she didn't get the cereal joke.

"You can't let Storm Novelo be on a team with Cameron, Edward, and I!" Lane insisted.

"Um ... actually," Storm said, "that would be 'with Cameron, Edward, and *me*.' Object of the preposition and all that."

Mr. Stovall dug into the pile of papers on his desk. "Lane, you should be thrilled to have Ms. Novelo join the team. She easily has the highest grade point in this class."

Storm couldn't help slumping in her chair.

"You're kidding," Lane said.

"And in her other classes, as well, I'd venture to say," Mr. Stovall continued. He handed Storm a stack of papers that looked like Quiz Bowl rules.

The bell rang, and kids bolted from the classroom before "Bones" had time to dismiss them.

Bridget detoured to pass by Lane. "Are you going to let Storm design new uniforms? This should be interesting. I might even show up for the big event."

Gracie and Annie stuck around with Storm, while Lane argued with Bones.

"But, but ...," Lane sputtered. "She won't take it seriously! She probably won't even show up for practices."

"Practices?" Storm thought she had enough going already with school, blog meetings, and her shifts at the supermarket. "You practice this stuff?"

"See?" Lane demanded. "I told you — !"

"That's cool," Storm said, forcing a smile. "When?"

"After school," Mr. Stovall answered.

"What day?" Storm asked.

"*Every* day!" Lane shouted.

Storm swallowed her surprise. "Cool. Filled with coolness."

"So just show up in the gym as soon as you can after school. All right, Storm?" Mr. Stovall shoved papers into his briefcase. "Glad to have you aboard." He walked out, whistling.

Lane opened her mouth, as if to say something else to Storm. Then she snapped it shut and left.

"You sure about this?" Annie asked weakly.

"She's sure," Gracie said. "It's written all over her face. You'll rock, Storm."

"Thanks, Gracie." Storm was grateful for the support. She needed it.

"Still doesn't mean you can be late for the blog meeting," Gracie warned, heading out. "Four thirty sharp!"

Storm hustled to her locker and repacked her backpack, hurried to the library, returned six library books, and checked out eight others — all loaded with facts that might come in handy for Quiz Bowl. Then she went straight to the gym.

The gym was deserted, and Storm thought she might be the first one there. Then she spotted four chairs set up onstage, three of them filled — with Lane, Cameron, and Edward Owen, a junior she barely knew by name.

She waved, amazed they could have gotten there so fast, then jogged up the steps to join them on center stage. "Why are we onstage?" It reminded her of the time she'd almost tried out for a part in the school play. That had been a big mistake. She hoped this wasn't another one.

When nobody answered Storm's question, Edward glanced from Cameron to Lane, then ventured, "This is where we sit for competitions. Cameron says sitting here for practices will help us not be nervous for competitions." Edward Owen was a junior, but he looked more like he was in junior high. He and Storm had never exchanged more than a smile — *her* smile, along with his look of surprise at her smile.

"We're onstage to help *you* not be nervous," Cameron corrected. "Some of us don't share your propensity for apprehension."

Storm wasn't exactly nervous, but she didn't feel like sitting. Instead, she paced in front of them. "This is tight. Could we get going, though. I can only stay an hour."

"See?" Lane said to Cameron. "Told you."

"What's wrong? What did I say?" Storm asked.

"This team is our highest priority," Cameron explained, without looking up from his notebook. "If you cannot share these priorities, I suggest you remove yourself from the team."

"Cameron," Storm said evenly, trying not to make things worse, "might as well face it, partner. I won't be 'removing myself from the team.' You've got me. Deal with it." That said, Storm took her seat. "Fire away, teammates! Let's bowl!"

Edward and Lane looked to see what Cameron would do. He took in several deep breaths. Still not looking directly at Storm, he handed her three thick books. "You should begin working with these quiz books on your own time."

"Cool!" Storm had never seen these titles before: *Facts and Figures, Quiz Bowl for the Competitor, Encyclopedic Knowledge at a Glance.* "I'll start reading them tonight — except maybe I'll just skim the one about facts and figures. Not that crazy about numbers. Math is my kryptonite, if you know what I mean."

"You can't just *read* the books," Cameron said, shaking his head.

"Why not?" Storm asked, thumbing through the top book.

"Because you have to study them," Lane answered. "Memorize things. Categorize them."

Storm knew she wouldn't have to do that. Reading was her ticket in. She'd always been able to remember what she read, especially if it interested her. But she decided not to argue. "Okay. So, roll 'em!" She glanced around for Bones. "Where's B — uh, Mr. Stovall?"

"He won't be joining us today," Cameron said. He opened a giant, old library book on his lap. "As captain of the Quiz Bowl team, I will be conducting today's practice. I'm going to toss out questions. You'll answer to the best of your abilities. And I'll take notes to report to Mr. Stovall."

Edward scooted to the edge of his chair, as if they'd be hurling themselves off the stage and racing through the gym. "Ready," he said.

Cameron held his book close to his face, probably so cheaters couldn't see the answers. "Which crop is the number-one crop raised in the United States?"

"Corn!" The word was out of Storm's mouth before she'd even thought about it. Before the others could open their mouths. She'd read a whole book about corn last year. "Corn's grown in the United States, like, twice as much as any other crop. But that could be because you can use it for almost anything — like vitamins and baby foods and condensed milk and peanut butter. And antibiotics! Plus, glue, and even chewing gum! You know what I think, though. What's going to keep our whole country from going crazy with gas prices like they are? Ethanol! Wave of the future, if you ask me." She sat back and waited for the next question.

"You can't do that," Lane said.

"Do what?" Storm had actually started thinking she might enjoy this whole thing after all.

"Spewing!" Lane exclaimed.

"Huh?" Storm still didn't get it.

Edward cleared his throat and explained, "Spewing is when a contestant throws in too much information. Judges could consider it showing off and develop a bias."

"More importantly," Cameron chimed in, "you risk losing the point. If you'd read the Quiz Bowl guidelines Mr. Stovall undoubtedly gave you, you'd know that Guideline Number Three is 'Be terse.' In our first contest, Edward buzzed in to answer the question, 'Who was our first divorced President?'

If he had simply answered 'Reagan,' or 'President Reagan,' we would have won the tournament. His expansive answer of 'Richard Reagan' instead of 'Ronald Reagan' lost us the first contest of the year."

"But what if he'd been right? Wouldn't the whole right answer be better for everybody than a half-right answer?" Storm really did want to know.

"See?" Lane said, turning to Cameron. "She's not going to play by the rules. I told you so. There's no way she's going to work out."

"Hello?" Storm said.

Still to Cameron, Lane insisted, "She's not intelligent enough to have on our team. She can't take it seriously. She'll ruin everything!"

"Right here!" Storm shouted, hating to be referred to in the third person, like she wasn't even there. "*She's* still on stage. Yoo-hoo!" Storm waved her hand in front of Lane's face.

Lane turned to frown directly at her.

"I get it," Storm said. "Terse. That's totally filled with grooviness and rightness. Moving right along. Hit us again, Cameron!"

The rest of the questions ranged from "Which U.S. city was the first to install a traffic light?" (Storm let Edward answer because she figured they all knew it was Cleveland.) to "What sport did Henry VIII and Queen Victoria love to play?" That one, Storm answered without thinking: "Archery." But her brain kicked in just in time to keep her from informing them, needlessly, that Henry started the first archery club, the Brotherhood of Saint George, in 1537.

She stayed at the practice as long as she could — longer than she should have — long enough to make her late for the blog meeting. Finally, she couldn't stand the thought of that disapproving look Gracie was so good at.

Storm hopped to her feet in the middle of another question that began, "What was the first of H.J. — ?"

"Horseradish," Storm answered, gathering her books into her arms because her pack was full.

"You need to let Cameron finish the question," Edward said.

Storm couldn't wait. "No time, Eddy. Besides, it had to be H.J. Heinz, right? Who else has those initials? Had to be a question about those fifty-seven varieties. Cameron said 'What was the *first* ...,' so the answer had to be horseradish. Which, by the way, is a great 3,000-year-old plant that's been used as an aphrodisiac, a cure for rheumatism, and a bitter herb for Passover seders. The United States produces six million gallons of the stuff a year, which is enough for sandwiches that could go twelve times around the earth, if anyone ever wanted to do that." She jerked her bag over her shoulder and stood up, wondering if she could carry this much without collapsing.

Her three teammates gazed at her with a mixture of disbelief and disdain.

Storm stopped a second and stared from one to the other. "Gotta bounce."

"Does that mean you're quitting?" Cameron asked.

Storm struggled to keep control. Cameron was leaning back in his chair. It would have been so easy to tip him over.

As soon as she got the thought, she could have kicked herself, tipped herself over. She was a Christian now. How could she think all of the stuff that ran through her head? "No, Cameron," she replied, smile in place. "I won't be quitting. You don't need to worry your pretty little head about that one. I'll be here tomorrow after school. And the day after that. And the day after that. And — "

"We get it," Lane muttered.

She cast one more smile on her fellow teammates. "Keep it real, guys! See you tomorrow."

Then as she exited, Storm let out a cry that echoed in the empty gymnasium: "Go BLHSQB!"

6

Storm's shoulders were aching from her load of books by the time she made it to Gracie's cottage. The white English-style cottage belonged to Gracie's real mother, who lived in London, Paris, New York, and just about everywhere except Big Lake, Ohio. It made the perfect spot for the blog team meetings, though — a whole lot better than on the stage of an empty gym.

The others were milling around the living room when Storm walked in. Gracie looked up first. "Storm Novelo!" she exclaimed, doing a bad job acting shocked to see Storm. "You know," Gracie continued, switching to the disappointed expression she'd mastered, "during our whole blog meeting, I kept thinking something was missing. Now I know what."

"You, Grace Doe, are filled with nastiness," Storm said, relieved that, despite the words, Gracie's grin made it clear she wasn't angry. "If you had any idea what I've been through with my *other* teammates, you would have greeted me with flowers and ice cream."

Mick the Munch, Gracie's stepsister, got off the couch and ran over to Storm. Mick was wearing her Cleveland Indians cap backward and her Indians shirt inside out. "Annie told me you joined the Quiz Bowl team, Storm. That's so fly! You'll totally rock!"

"Thanks, Mick. You're the only one who thinks so," Storm replied, heading for the big easy chair. They'd nicknamed the cushy leather recliner "Gracie's throne" because she demanded to sit in it for their blog meetings. Storm loved to steal the chair whenever she could, just to get Gracie's random reaction.

The minute Storm plopped into the comfy chair, it struck her that this was one more *wrong* thing she did automatically. Why? Why couldn't she be automatically sweet and good, like Mick? Storm changed seats and plopped next to Jazz on the couch.

"I give up," Gracie said, sliding back onto her throne. "Why aren't you hogging my chair?"

"It's a long story," Storm said. "And I wouldn't want to be accused of 'spewing.'"

Jazz scooted farther away from her on the couch. "Thanks for the warning."

Annie had been sitting at the computer across the room. "I think this will be one of the best blogs we've ever had on *That's What You Think!* Especially after Mick posts Storm's blog."

Storm had almost forgotten about her "Didyanose" blog. But at least she had the piece handwritten. She pulled it out of her backpack. "I'll just type it in when you're done, okay?" She still had to find out this week's theme so she could do some kind of tie-in. "Annie, why don't you read some of your 'Professor Love' blog? And some of Gracie's blog too?"

"Sweet!" Annie exclaimed. "Thought you'd never ask. I'll start with Gracie's."

Storm joined Annie at the computer because she'd always rather read herself than be read to.

. . . .

THAT'S WHAT YOU THINK!

by Jane

MAY 27

SUBJECT: REGRETS

Can you believe another school year is almost gone? We'll never get it back. True, almost everybody at Typical High seems to be in celebration mode over the closing of another year. But I've observed other, more subtle reactions, gestures, and body language that tell me most people have regrets.

Have you measured up to your own vision for the year? Were you the person you thought you'd be?

Admit it. The day before school started, didn't you have big plans? Hopes? Weren't you going to change your life?

How did that go for you? Are you the person you wanted to be? Any regrets?

Here are some cues I've observed this week at Typical High:

- *lip biting, mouth tightening*

- *subtle shakes of the head*

- *failure to look anyone in the eyes*

- *exhaling air that didn't appear to have been inhaled*

- *turning away from certain conversations, tuning out others*

Have you ever said any of these things to yourself?

I wish I had that to do over again.

Why did I say that? Why didn't I say that?

Sure would be nice to be able to take that back, to rewind the year and undo that thing I did.

Wish I'd followed through with that.

What was I thinking?!

Storm laughed, and Annie stopped reading. "Sorry," Storm said.

"What is it?" Annie asked.

"Nothing. Keep reading, Annie." But what had made Storm laugh was the fact that she'd said every one of those comments to herself over the past week. Maybe during the past twenty-four hours. She'd had such high hopes for herself after she'd become a Christian, but she kept messing up.

Annie read on, and Storm sat back down on the couch and looked over her food notes. They didn't have much to do with regret, so she added a couple of facts about weight gain and obese Americans and made a clumsy tie-in to the theme of regret. It would have to do.

When she tuned in to what Annie was reading, Storm wasn't sure if the blog was Gracie's or Annie's. Usually, Annie wrote about love. This blog seemed to be about love, but the description of body language must have come straight from Gracie.

"So," Annie was saying, reading from the computer screen, "if you can read a guy's or a girl's body language, you'll know

if that person really wants to be 'just friends,' or if he has
something much more in mind. This can save you from doing
or saying things you'll later regret.

"Here are some signs you can look for in the person you'd
like to become special:

Cute-puppy Shoulder Move: If a guy lifts his shoulders, like
you would if you saw cute puppies and said 'Oooh! They're so
cute!' then the guy likes you. So if you like him, you probably
won't regret striking up a conversation with him.

Hands-up Winner (Hands-down Loser): Watch the guy's hands
as he talks to you. If he gestures palms up, you've got yourself
a winner — someone willing to be vulnerable. Maybe. At least
you might not regret it if you make the first move.

Bows, Brows & Wows: While she's talking to you, she bows
her head ever so slightly and gazes up at you, as if peeking
from under those big, thick lashes. She might as well be
writing her phone number on the back of your hand! Call her,
and you just might not regret it.

Pigeon-toed, Pretty-please Move: If she turns in her toes, like a
shy little kid would do, she is so into you. On the other hand,
if you see those toes out and hands behind the back, military
style, step away from the girl! Try to get her to give you the
time of day, and you might add that move to your list of regrets."

Annie stopped reading and smiled over at Jazz and Storm.
"You probably guessed that Gracie gave me all the body-
language clues," Annie admitted. "It was fun working it out
together, wasn't it Gracie?"

"Just so long as we're straight that Annie came up with her
own names for these signals," Gracie said.

Jazz grinned. "And all the time I thought 'Cute-puppy' move was so Gracie."

Storm loved Jazz's dry wit. It never came off mean, especially since Jazz had become a Christian. Storm had already noticed changes in her friend, and Jazz hadn't even been a believer as long as she had.

The meeting broke up, and Storm took over at the computer. She typed in her food facts and wished she'd been paying better attention when they'd decided on the theme.

"Ready for me?" Mick asked. Mick, Gracie's stepsister, was only in seventh grade, but everything techy about the website fell to her. She never complained. Mick made sure not just anybody could post things on their site. She'd created a password, so everything had to go through her. You couldn't play it too safe on the Internet, Gracie always said. No personal info. No real names.

Storm moved over so Mick could get started.

Mick began keying in the codes, but she glanced at Storm. "You okay, Storm?"

Storm shrugged.

"How's that Bible working out?"

Storm slapped her forehead. "I can't believe I forgot to read it again this morning!" Gracie and Mick had given her a cool Bible. Storm had promised herself that she'd read a chapter of the New Testament every day, but she'd forgotten more times than she'd remembered. "I really want to read the whole Bible," she complained. "At this rate, I'll be a hundred eleven before I get to Revelation."

"Don't be so hard on yourself," Mick said. She hit "control something" and Storm's entire blog appeared on the *That's*

What You Think! website. Storm felt bad that her blog didn't really fit in with the others.

"I keep messing up, Mick," Storm complained. "I want to say grace before meals, read the Bible, and pray more. But I don't. And I don't want to keep mouthing off or having lies slip out before I get a chance to stop them — or a hundred other things I do and don't do — "

"Storm." Mick was grinning at her.

"Are you not getting what I'm saying, Mick?" Storm wondered if feeling like this was so far out of Mick's experience that she couldn't understand.

"Read the verse I posted for this week," Mick said, scrolling to the end of the blogs. "Here." She stood up and turned the computer chair back to Storm. "Paul wrote that, Storm. As in the apostle Paul."

Storm sat on the edge of the computer seat and read the verses:

> *"I do not understand what I do. For what I want to do I do not do, but what I hate I do. . . . For I have the desire to do what is good, but I cannot carry it out. For what I do is not the good I want to do; no, the evil I do not want to do — this I keep on doing. . . . What a wretched man I am! Who will rescue me from this body of death? Thanks be to God — through Jesus Christ our Lord!" Romans 7:15, 18 – 19, 24 – 25 (But read the whole chapter! Next one too!)*

"Storm?" Jazz said. Storm didn't know how long Jazz had been standing there. "You all right? What were you reading?"

Storm stared up at Jazz. "My diary."

7

"You were reading your diary?" Jazz clarified.

"I might as well have been," Storm answered. The phrases in the verses chased each other in her head: *What I want to do, I don't do. I do what I hate. I have the desire to do what is good, but I cannot carry it out.*

"Okay," Jazz said, obviously not getting it. "I guess that's what blogging is, right? Like a diary, only you let a bunch of strangers read it. No lock and key." Jazz didn't blog. She just did a cartoon for the website.

Not "just" a cartoon. Storm knew nobody could, week after week, come up with great drawings and funny stuff like Jazz did. Last week when Gracie had blogged about after-school jobs, Jazz had drawn a picture of a teen stretched out in a hammock. Her mother was obviously screaming at her. The caption read, "Mother: Hard work never killed anybody! Daughter: Yeah? Well, I'm not taking any chances."

This week, she'd sketched a scene of penguins posing for a picture in Antarctica. A skunk was taking the penguins' picture and saying, "I knew I shouldn't have spent that extra money on color film." She'd titled it "Even Skunks Have Stinkin' Regrets."

"Are you guys talking about diaries?" Annie asked. "I used to keep one."

"Now there's a diary I'd like to read," Gracie commented.

They fell into a discussion about diaries and blogs and instant messaging and chat rooms, and how it used to be a lot safer when people had the only key to their diaries. Storm didn't join in on the conversation. She kept coming back to the verses.

Annie offered to give her a ride home, but Storm passed. It wasn't far. Besides, she needed to get by herself and think. Those verses had done something inside of her. The words felt alive. She wanted to walk and turn over the thoughts in her head. She wanted to zero in on that last part, where Paul thanked God in Christ for getting him out of *his* funk.

She'd barely gotten to the end of the drive, when she heard Jazz calling after her. "Hang on a minute!" Tall and lithe, Jazz Fletcher looked graceful even when tiptoeing down the gravel drive.

"You walking my way?" Storm asked, waiting for Jazz.

Jazz shook her head. "Not yet. I just wanted to ask you about your dad."

Storm's stomach tightened. "My dad?"

"Yeah. Is he okay?"

Storm glared up at Jazz, who towered over her. "Why? Did Annie say something to you about Dad?" Storm had confided in Annie. Annie never should have told Jazz about Dad's depression. Couldn't she keep her big mouth shut?

"Annie?" Jazz looked confused. "Why would I talk to Annie about your dad?"

Immediately, Storm felt guilty. Why did she always react like that? She should have known she could trust Annie. Annie wouldn't have run to Jazz behind her back and gossiped about Storm's dad. And anyway, so what if Jazz did know about Dad's depression. "Sorry."

"I just wondered if he's sick. He didn't do the lawn over the weekend. Or today. Not that I care," Jazz added quickly. "If you ask me, our grass is fine the way it is."

"Dad didn't mow your lawn?" Storm knew that he always did that neighborhood first on Saturday. This was Tuesday. The Fletchers lived in the most expensive part of town. Since her dad had been mowing for Jazz's family, he'd picked up other clients in the same neighborhood.

"It's not a big deal. I was just afraid he was sick or something. Anyway ..." Jazz turned to go back to the cottage. "See you later?"

"Wait a minute," Storm said. "Please?" It was stupid of her to hide her feelings from Jazz. That's what the old Storm would have done — pretended everything was just fine. But Storm didn't want to play those games. Not anymore. "Dad's not sick. At least, not that way. Got a minute?"

Storm and Jazz sat on the curb under the big maple at the foot of the cottage drive. After a couple of minutes stalling, Storm confided in Jazz and asked her to pray for her dad and for his depression.

Jazz listened. She always listened without interrupting. Storm appreciated that. Jazz didn't say much when Storm was finished. But when she said, "I'll pray for your dad, Storm," Storm felt better. She knew Jazz really would.

Storm was surprised to see her dad's lawn truck still in the driveway when she got home. All the equipment was loaded. Maybe he'd gotten his work done and come home early.

But as she walked into the house, Storm didn't think that was the explanation. "Dad? Hello?"

There was no answer. She dropped her backpack and walked out to the greenhouse. "Dad? You home?"

Still no answer. Storm heard the humming of the sewing machine coming from her bedroom. She backtracked, knowing she'd find her mother hunkered over the little sewing machine.

Her mother glanced up but kept on working. "I told Mrs. Russell I'd have this finished today. But I have the evening shift at the supermarket. They're keeping customer service open later and later."

"How come Dad's truck is in the driveway?" Storm asked.

"Because he's home."

"Where is he?" Storm asked.

"Sleeping." She revved the sewing machine again, making it sound angry.

"But what about his lawns?" Storm asked.

The sewing stopped. "What lawns?"

"He hasn't mowed Jazz's lawn yet," Storm said. "The Fletchers?"

Her mother's eyes grew hard. "He hasn't? What about the others in that neighborhood?"

Storm felt like she was ratting out her dad. She hadn't meant to. She thought her mother would have known about the unmown lawns. Her mom kept track of everything.

"I don't know about the other lawns," Storm said. But

she couldn't imagine that he'd do other lawns in that
neighborhood and not do the Fletchers'.

Storm's mother stood up and moved past Storm with the
swiftness of a striking snake. She slithered through the maze
of clothes hanging around the room and closed the door
behind her.

Storm could hear her parents' voices through the closed
doors. Her mother and father never fought, or at least not that
she heard. Until now. Now, her mother's shouts were coming
through loud and clear.

"What are we supposed to do, Eddy?" she asked. "You can't
keep this up!"

Her father's voice sounded muffled. Storm couldn't make
out the words.

Suddenly, her mother bolted out of the bedroom and
shouted, "Storm! Change your clothes and get out here!
You're coming with me!"

By the time Storm changed, her mom was sitting behind
the wheel of the old pickup, motor running. The gears ground
as she tried to get the truck to reverse. "Get in!" Mom hollered.

Storm got in as the gears screeched again. "Mom, have you
ever driven the truck?"

"No," Mom admitted.

"Do you know how?"

"Not yet." Mom stared at the little diagram on the gearshift
and tried to shift gears again. The truck sounded like it
needed oiling, but it jerked backward and then let Mom back
it down the driveway.

It took three tries, but Mom finally got the thing to go
forward and creep up to the highway. All they had to do was

cross the highway and turn up a few streets, but it must have taken them fifteen minutes because Storm's mother couldn't find second gear.

When she stopped in front of the Fletchers' house, the truck shut off all by itself. "Good," Mom muttered.

They worked together to get the newer mower out of the truck. Storm's dad always used a gas push mower, except when he mowed for the Spiels' Corporation. Jazz's dad had gotten him that job too. Spiels had their own lawn mowers, and Storm's dad loved driving the riding mower. He claimed he didn't want one himself because he could do a better job with a push mower, but Storm suspected he just plain couldn't afford his own riding mower.

She tried not to think about her dad. He had to be pretty bad off to let his best client's lawn get this long. But he really had to be in bad shape to let his wife take care of it. Storm's dad treated her mom like a princess. That's what he called her, "my little princess." That's what she was too. She descended from a long line of Mayan royalty.

Unfortunately for Storm and her mother, that Mayan royalty line was so long that the royal coffers had been emptied generations ago.

Storm's mother gassed up the mower, while Storm got out rakes and lawn trimmers. "I'll mow," Mom announced, starting the mower on the first try. "Start with the weeds!" she shouted.

It had been a long time since Storm had helped with the lawns. When she was little, she loved following her dad around when he was working. But by the time she started middle school, Storm hadn't wanted to have anything to do with lawn care.

She pulled on white cotton gloves and walked to the main
sidewalk in search of weeds, hoping she'd remember what to
do with them when she found them.

8

Storm was squinting over a long, scraggly green thing, trying to decide if it was grass or weed, when she heard a door slam. She looked up to see Jazz bounding down the front steps. Jazz was wearing black thigh-high shorts with a cool top Storm knew she'd designed and made herself. She looked tight.

"I'll start at this end!" Jazz called, squatting over weeds that stuck out of the neatly cropped bushes at one end of the sidewalk.

"You don't need to do this," Storm shouted down to her.

Jazz ignored the comment.

After about fifteen minutes, Ty, Jazz's little brother, came running up to Storm. Ty and Mick were best buddies, and they both played baseball for the middle school. Waving both hands like he planned on bringing in a battalion of fighter planes, Ty jumped in front of Storm's mother.

Mom stopped. The mower died. "Can I help you?" Storm's mom asked, her voice clipped.

Ty grinned at Storm's mom. "You took the words right out of my mouth," he said, reaching for the mower.

Storm could tell that her mother still didn't understand. "Excuse me, but I need to get back to work."

"No you don't," Ty said, stepping behind the mower. "I'd really like to mow. You'd be doing me a favor. I used to get to mow the lawn all the time. I miss it."

"Are you sure, Ty?" Storm asked.

Her mother reached for the mower. "I can't let you do this."

Storm could see how hard it was for her mom to accept help. Then she remembered that her dad had two mowers. He hadn't been able to let the old one go when he got the new one. He said he'd need it one day, when he had dozens of people working for him.

"Mom," Storm tried. "Why don't you let Ty use this mower, and I'll get you the other mower. It will go twice as fast. You'll have to leave pretty soon anyway if you don't want to be late to the supermarket."

Her mother glanced at her watch, and Storm knew she was worried about making her shift. "Well ..."

The mower roared to life, and Ty took off at a jog.

The Fletchers' lawn was huge. But with all of them working, Storm thought it was going pretty fast. Gracie came by, picked up the rake, and started in without a word to anybody.

A few minutes later, Mick showed up and seemed to know how to trim the grass by the walks better than any of them. "Isn't it amazing how fast grass grows!" she exclaimed, tugging at a weed with both hands.

"You're so easily amused, Mick," Gracie teased.

But Storm was thinking Mick had a point. Storm had read about state grasses. Only fourteen states had one. They had cool names, like "blue grama" for Colorado; "Indian grass" for Oklahoma; and "big bluestem" for Illinois. The thing they all had in common was that they grew like crazy.

"So why does grass grow like that?" Storm asked. "*How* does grass grow anyway?" She couldn't ever remember reading much about how grass grew. Or why.

"That's easy," Mick answered. "People can water grass and fertilize it, but they can't make it grow. Only God can do that."

Storm loved the way Mick thought and talked. Christ was such a big part of her life that answers like that came out of her naturally. Storm wondered if she would ever be like that.

She was starting to think that they could actually pull off the lawn job, when her mother came up behind her and whispered, "We have to do at least one more lawn tonight."

"Tonight?" Storm couldn't believe it. She'd been picturing how terrific a nice, hot bath would feel as soon as they finished off this lawn.

"We can't lose our newer customers, Storm," Mom said, her voice low and urgent. "I'm going to the house two doors down. According to your father's books, that's one of ours." She pointed across the street. "And those two."

"I'm so tired!" Storm complained.

Her mom glanced away, as if checking the sky for signs.

Storm hated herself for complaining. What was wrong with her? Her mom must be twice as tired, and she still had a shift at the supermarket to get through. "You should go home and get cleaned up, Mom. You don't want to be late. I'll make sure we finish the other lawn on this side of the street. Okay?"

"I can't leave," her mom said.

"Don't worry, Mrs. Novelo," Mick chimed in. She was pulling weeds a couple of feet away. "Sorry. I didn't mean to eavesdrop. But we'll all help Storm get that other yard done. It will be okay."

"I can't ask you to — "

"You're not asking," Gracie said. She had dirt smudged across her forehead and dirt on her jeans and T-shirt. "Go. We'll take it from here."

Storm's mother seemed to be weakening. Then her gaze moved to Ty and the lawnmower. "But the equipment? It's kind of you to offer, but — "

"We'll store stuff in our shed," Jazz suggested. "Then it will be here for the other lawns."

Storm hadn't said anything, but she felt like crying. That's how proud she was to have friends like these. She knew her mom would be too grateful, too indebted, to say more. "Go, Mom," she said.

Her mother nodded, lips pressed tightly together. Then she ran for the truck and drove away.

Everybody started gathering rakes, hoes, and mowers.

"You guys," Storm began. "Thanks. I don't know what we'd do if — "

Nobody paid any attention to her. Instead, they started up the sidewalk, as if they were lining up for a lawn-care parade.

"You're really — !" Storm shouted after them.

Only Gracie turned around. "Storm Novelo," she called, "are you going to get back to work, or what?"

Storm wanted to be like all of them when she grew up.

They stopped three houses down from the Fletchers' house, at the lawn Storm's mom had pointed out. The house was set back from the road and was the biggest house on the block, except for Jazz's. Storm didn't like it as much as she liked the Fletchers' house. The big turrets and gables seemed out of place, and the perfectly aligned white bricks weren't half as cool as the Fletchers' rough-hewn stone walls.

"We better hurry!" Jazz hollered, taking over the old mower Storm's mom had used. "We're going to run out of light."

The sun sank faster than Storm had expected, making it harder than ever to tell the weeds from the flowers and grass. They stuck with it, though, until the entire front lawn was mowed, sidewalks trimmed, and weeds — hopefully — pulled.

Stars sneaked out, and lightning bugs flashed, as they gathered up the equipment and headed back to Jazz's. Storm wasn't sure she'd ever felt this tired.

"Hey! Where do you think you're going?" someone shouted. A figure stomped out of the white brick house, yelling and waving them back. "Get back here!"

Storm squinted. All she could make out was the dark figure of some guy. But there was something familiar about that voice.

They all stayed where they were and waited for him. As he got closer, the sick feeling in Storm's stomach grew sicker. "Wait," she muttered. "Huh-uh. No way."

But there he was. Large as life.

Cameron Worthington the Third.

9

"Cameron?" Storm cried. "What are *you* doing here?"

"This is my house!" Cameron answered, pointing out the white brick monstrosity.

Storm wheeled on Jazz. "Jasmine Fletcher, did you know we were mowing Cameron's yard?"

"Thought it might be a good idea to keep that one to myself as long as possible," Jazz admitted.

Cameron frowned at all of them equally, as if he didn't recognize his *teammate*. "Where's that Mexican guy?"

Storm wanted to hit him over the head with her rake. "That Mexican guy? Do you mean my father, you — ?"

Jazz interrupted just in time. "Cameron, it's late. Mr. Novelo hasn't been well, and we're helping him out. I'm sure you understand."

"We have a backyard, you know," Cameron informed them, not responding to Jazz's information about Storm's father. "A very sizeable backyard," he added.

"Well, bully for you," Storm muttered.

"Hey, man," Ty said. "We'll catch you tomorrow. No problem." Ty moved off, and the rest of Storm's friends followed, with Gracie tugging on Storm's arm to make her come with them.

Storm fully intended to read her Quiz Bowl books when she got back home. But after soaking in the tub and getting ready for bed, she fell asleep without cracking a book.

When Storm got to school the next day, all she could think about was Quiz Bowl practice and showing up Cameron. So even though she'd promised herself that she'd pay attention in her classes, she just couldn't. Instead of listening to her art teacher, Storm kept peeking into the fact books.

By English class, she could see that her study methods weren't working for Quiz Bowl preparation. Bones had coached her on the best way to absorb information that might come up in competition. She was supposed to pick the main points of each subject category and move ahead.

But Storm just couldn't do it. She kept getting intrigued by bits of information that led her down side paths, away from quiz material. When she tried to make a list of recent Oscar winners because she thought that might make a good question, she got sidetracked into reading all about one director's family and how they'd moved to France and grown water lilies. Then she'd wondered about water lilies. And before she realized it, she was reading all about them, even though she couldn't imagine a question coming up about water lilies at competition.

After history class, Storm skipped going to her locker and raced to the gym. Still, she was the last one to climb the stage and take her seat.

"Finally," Lane muttered. "Cameron," she went on, as if Storm hadn't arrived at all, "if she can't make practices on time, maybe we should get someone else."

"Who, for example?" Storm asked, settling into her stage seat. "I don't see people lining up to join our team. Do you?"

"Amanda Rogers would join," Lane snapped.

Storm knew Lane and Amanda were tight. But Storm had English with Amanda and had never once heard her answer a question in class. At least, not correctly.

"Why would you want Amanda on the team?" Edward asked. "She's failing American history."

Storm thought about hugging him, but decided against it.

Mr. Stovall walked up and sat on a wooden stool he pulled over from stage left. "Glad to see you're all here on time," he began. The comment made Storm wonder if Cameron had reported her as showing up late last time.

Bones gave Storm an especially warm smile, a sympathizing smile, Storm thought. He cleared his throat. "Storm, I hope you weren't too discouraged yesterday."

"Excuse me?" she asked, trying to think of any discouraging moments he might have heard about.

"Cameron told me about your first practice, and you shouldn't let it get you down."

Storm glared over at Cameron, but he was thumbing through his notes, obviously pretending not to notice her. "Cameron told you about our practice?" she asked, turning back to Bones.

"He said it was pretty rough," Bones continued. "But we don't want you to get down about it. Right, team?"

Storm felt like screaming that she'd answered more of Cameron's little quiz questions than the others combined, that she'd held back so they could answer some, that Cameron was an insecure stupidhead.

"But I think you'll have a better time of it today," Bones went on. "Cameron suggested we focus on questions from another area, one I think you confided to him was your favorite."

Storm was baffled. She'd sooner pull out her fingernails and eyelashes than confide anything to Cameron Worthington the Third. "My favorite area?"

"Mathematics." Bones said it as if he were tempting her with chocolate chip cookies.

Math was the only area Storm wasn't really interested in, and Cameron knew it. Storm had let it slip, calling numbers her kryptonite, and he'd pounced on it like Lex Luthor.

"Cameron ..." Storm stopped herself before saying what she was thinking. "Cameron must have misunderstood me."

"No. I definitely heard her say it," Lane seconded.

"Well, it's always good to practice our math questions," Bones said. "Let's get started, shall we?"

Storm had trouble focusing on the questions because she was too busy trying to count to ten so she wouldn't explode at Lane and Cameron. Besides, there was nothing spectacular about numbers. She kind of liked geometry because you got to figure things out, but algebra was a bore. And word problems could be interesting. Too interesting. Like when Mr. Stovall began, "If Ella and Samuel rode a train from Paris to Vienna, and it took them eight hours ...," Storm would be stuck back with Ella and Samuel on that train and remember a book she'd read about trains. And she'd start thinking about station names and that the shortest train station name was *Ib*, near Jharsuguda on the Howrah-Nagpur main line South Eastern Railway, India. And then she'd remember reading about a "cowcatcher" once and then looking it up and finding out that's what they called the big metal grill on the front of trains.

And by that time, she'd have missed hearing two more questions.

Storm only answered one question during quiz practice. Edward answered two. Lane and Cameron answered all the rest.

"Well, it's only our second practice," Bones said.

"But we only have two more practices before competition," Lane whined.

Bones put on a brave front, saying he knew the team would get stronger. But Storm studied his face and thought of Annie's and Gracie's blogs on regret. *Mouth tight. Biting of the lip. Subtle shake of head. Failure to look directly into anyone's eyes.*

Poor Bones. He showed every single sign of regret, regret that he'd ever let Storm Novelo on the Quiz Bowl team.

10

Storm had almost made it out of the auditorium, when Cameron called after her, "Tell your dad not to bother working on our lawn next week. We'll be finding somebody we can depend on."

Storm seethed inside. She stopped. Turned. And with the best smile she could muster, she shouted back at Cameron, "Super, Cameron! I'll tell him. He'll be glad to hear it too, you ... you ... you loser. My dad is much too busy to mow the lawns of losers."

Mick was waiting for Storm in the hall outside the gym.

"Mick!" Storm exclaimed, unreasonably glad to see her.

"Thought you might want somebody to walk with," Mick said.

"You wouldn't even believe what I've been through!" Storm said, still fuming. She wanted to get out of there as fast as she could. "Cameron is so underhanded!" What hurt the most, though, she thought as they stepped outside under gray skies, was Cameron's crack about her dad not being dependable. "Cameron Worthington the Third is so ... so filled with nastiness!" Her heart pounded harder with every step down the sidewalk. "And meanness. And heartlessness."

Most of her other friends would have chimed in about now. Annie would have expressed outrage. Jazz would have come up with something appropriately cutting to say about Cameron. Gracie would have at least come through with grunts of agreement.

Not Mick. She just seemed to frown deeper, her forehead wrinkling.

"He slammed my dad, Mick!" Storm explained. "My dad, who's hanging on the best he can. Cameron never even bothered to ask me why my dad didn't show up to work on his stupid lawn. Not even once did he ask *why*!"

Mick still didn't say anything. Storm walked faster and faster, going over every hateful word Cameron had said, every underhanded thing he'd done to her.

"I wonder why he's like that?" Mick said at last, her voice so soft that Storm wasn't sure she'd heard right. "You mean Dad? Why he's like he is?"

"No. Cameron. I wonder why he's like that. Why would he attack your dad? And you? He has to know how smart you are. Why would he go to the trouble of trying to get you off the team? Or mess you up by saying things about your dad? He must be one sad guy, huh? I don't think I've ever seen Cameron when Ty and I've played ball over there. I've never seen him playing catch with his dad or anything."

Storm glanced over at Mick. She could tell Mick hadn't meant anything except what she'd said. Mick had honestly been wondering about Cameron, trying to understand why he was like he was.

And Storm hadn't been wondering anything of the kind. It was exactly what Storm had nailed Cameron for, not even asking why her dad hadn't shown up for work. Yet Storm hadn't once thought about why Cameron was like he was. The question had never entered her mind.

Lord, she prayed, *when am I going to be like Mick? Ever? I'm sorry I let Cameron get to me like that. It would be so great if you'd change me.*

Mick had already changed the subject. "Gracie's meeting us by Jazz's so we can finish the lawns. Ty and Jazz should be there already. Annie's coming as soon as she can break away from the shop."

"Mick, I called Cameron a loser," Storm admitted.

Mick didn't say anything.

Storm wondered if Mick had ever called anybody a name. She thought about Romans 7. The night before, she'd read the whole chapter, and this morning she'd read Romans 8. She'd felt like that letter to the Romans could have been a letter to Storm or maybe a letter *from* Storm. She'd prayed as she read, letting the words sink into her.

And yet here she was, acting just like she always had. "I am such a lousy Christian."

"You are not!" Mick protested. Then she added, "Well, I guess we all are, when it comes down to it. The only really great Christian was Jesus."

When they got to Cameron's house, Storm's mother and Ty came strolling from the backyard.

"We're finished with this one," said her mom, smiling.

"Sweet!" Mick exclaimed.

They moved across the street and started in on the other lawns. By the end, they'd developed a system and knew what to do without consulting at every turn. They finished her dad's other lawns before dark.

This time, Storm's mother thanked each of Storm's friends individually. She offered to pay them, but they laughed her off.

It was dark by the time Storm and her mom finished putting away the mowing equipment. When they walked into the house, the lights were out. Storm stepped on something. She picked it up. "Dad's slipper," she muttered.

Storm's mother turned on the lights, then flitted around the living room picking up candy-bar wrappers, empty water bottles, and stray socks. "I've had it!" she said.

Storm slipped off to her bedroom and tried to shut out the voices coming from her parents' room.

Thursday's Quiz Bowl practice felt more like a war than a competition, but Storm was determined to stick with it. She still needed to tell her parents she was competing. So on Friday morning, she got up early and tiptoed to her parents' bedroom, rehearsing what she'd say.

Only her dad was still in bed. He was curled up, facing the wall. She just couldn't talk to him. Not today.

Quiz Bowl practice wasn't too bad. Bones seemed genuinely surprised when she crushed on the English and science categories. Storm hadn't kept tract, but she was pretty sure she'd gotten more answers right than Cameron. Once, when he blew a question about DNA and she got it right, she saw him wince. And in spite of herself, she heard Mick's question in her head: *Why is Cameron like that?*

Since she didn't have lawns to mow or a blog meeting to get to, Storm stayed for the whole practice.

"Good job, everybody!" Mr. Stovall said, when they'd been quizzed on each category. The tight mouth and other signs of regret had vanished from Bones's face. "I think we have a real

shot at winning the trophy at competition next Saturday. I
hope you've invited your family and friends to come and cheer
for you."

Storm felt a guilt twinge about not having told her mom,
at least, about Quiz Bowl. She hadn't lied, but she'd let
her mother think she'd been hanging out with friends after
school. Again, it struck Storm how easy it was for her to live
like she'd always lived, deceiving her parents, conveniently
deeming those "little" lies as "white." She needed to tell both
of her parents about Quiz Bowl, and soon.

As she left the gym, she tried to think of a way she could
get through to her dad.

"You've got lots of friends who will come and cheer for you,
don't you." Edward was following her, and she hadn't even
noticed he was there.

"What?" Storm had to replay his words in her head.
"Yeah. I guess. I don't know if they'll *cheer*." She smiled back at
Edward.

He jerked his head down and seemed to study his shoes.
Storm hadn't really noticed how shy he was.

"You're really good with geography questions, Eddy —
Edward," she said, correcting herself before he could.

Edward glanced at her, and Storm thought his eyes, at
least, were smiling. "Someday I'm going to be a pilot and fly
to every country in the world."

"Far out!" Storm never would have guessed the kid trailing
behind her would have a dream like that. "That's so tight,
Edward! You'll do it too. I have no doubts."

He shrugged. "I have it all planned. I'm going to get
a scholarship to the University of Colorado. I'll study

aerodynamics and geography and start my flight training while I'm still at the university."

"Man, Edward!" She stopped, so he had to come up and walk beside her instead of following her. "I can't even see past my freshman year, and that's just one more week."

He looked down again.

"Good for you, guy!" she said, elbowing him.

Edward did grin this time. And the grin lit up a face Storm had barely noticed before. It was a classically handsome face, with bone structure Storm would be sure to tell Jazz, the artist, about.

"See you Monday!" Edward called, doing a U-turn and heading back the way they'd come.

Storm was still thinking about Edward and wondering what his family was like, when she arrived home. She walked inside, hoping to find her parents together so she could tell them about Quiz Bowl. She started to holler for them, but stopped when she heard them arguing.

"If you can't do your job, can't you at least pick up around here?" Storm's mother's voice filled the whole house. "I'm working customer service. I'm doing your work on the lawns. I'm sewing and doing alterations when I'm home. And you can't even pick up after yourself? I can't go on like this!"

Storm knew everything her mother said was true. But she ached for her father. He was a hard worker all year long. Why couldn't he just snap himself out of it? She wanted to tell him about the varsity letter, to give him something to think about that didn't make him so sad.

But what if he counted on this letter, and she didn't come through with one? She knew Mr. Stovall would bend all the rules he could to see that she got one. But if she totally struck out in competition, he couldn't claim she'd really lettered in Quiz Bowl.

And besides, how could she talk to her dad about this stuff? She hadn't been able to talk to him about anything for weeks.

Storm missed her dad. It was as if he'd gone away to a desert, where plants didn't grow, and where she couldn't go. All she wanted was to do something that would bring him back.

11

Saturday, Storm couldn't stop checking the clock during her shift at Big Lake Foods. Usually, she enjoyed her bagging job because she got to visit with customers. She loved entertaining people with trivia about the food they were buying. But this morning, she had to struggle to think of things to say.

"What's the matter, Stormy?" asked a woman who always misread Storm's nametag. The elderly woman was one of the few people Storm let get away with calling her "Stormy." She shopped every Saturday and always came through Storm's line, no matter how busy it was. "No peach facts this morning?" She sounded disappointed.

Storm placed each peach into a brown bag and tried to think of something. "Peaches belong to the rose family," she said.

"You told me that before," the woman replied, taking her little bag of hard, fuzzless peaches.

"Sorry. Have a nice day?" Storm hated disappointing customers, but it was taking everything she had just to bag their groceries. It occurred to her that maybe this was what her dad felt like. Only much worse. Like everything was such an effort that nothing seemed worth it.

"Rough day?" Tammy Jo asked. TJ was supposed to be the toughest cashier in town, but Storm loved her. Storm had bagged for TJ since the first day she'd signed on at Big Lake Foods.

"Rough week," Storm admitted.

"Why don't you knock off for a few minutes? Take a break. I can handle things until you get back. Maybe your mom could use a break too."

"Thanks, TJ" Storm walked over to the little customer-service counter, where her mom had worked for a couple of weeks now. The customer-service booth was set apart from the regular checkout, a high, box-shaped office, with walls that only came up halfway.

Storm started to wave, then saw that her mom was with a customer. A tall guy was leaning on the counter, pointing his finger in her mom's face, while her mother listened stoically to his complaints. It took a second for Storm to realize the guy was Cameron.

Her first thought was that she was caught in some kind of recurring nightmare starring Cameron Worthington the Third. Her second thought was to bend back the finger he was sticking in her mother's face.

"I want my money back. I'm not going to drink spoiled milk!" Cameron plopped a gallon milk jug onto the customer-service counter. The smack made several customers turn to look.

"The purchase date would make the milk fresh for another week or more," Storm's mother explained, pointing to the stamped date on the jug. "When did you purchase it?"

"I don't have to answer to you," Cameron snapped. "I want to see the manager."

"I'm so sorry," she said patiently. "The manager won't be in
until later this evening. You're welcome to — "

"I demand a refund now!" Cameron insisted.

Storm couldn't believe it. He'd probably left the milk in his
car overnight. And even if he hadn't, big deal. His family had
enough money to buy the whole milk company. She'd like to
pour that jug of spoiled milk right over his head and —

She stopped. *Sorry, God. There I go again.*

At least she hadn't actually done it. "Hey, Cameron! How's
it going?"

Cameron looked surprised to see her. "I knew you worked
here," he said, as if it had been something she'd tried to keep
secret from him. "And I'll tell you how it's going. It's not going
well. That's how it's going. This woman here refuses to give
me a refund."

"Sir, please," her mother pleaded. "You misunderstood.
Of course, you can have a refund. We like to ask the
circumstances so it won't happen again. That's all."

Cameron smirked at Storm. "These people will say anything."

Storm waited until she could control her voice. "Cameron,
I'd like you to meet one of 'these people.' 'This woman' is Mrs.
Novelo."

He frowned from one Novelo to the other.

"Here's your refund," said Storm's mother, handing him
his money. "Sorry for your inconvenience. Thank you for
shopping at Big Lake Foods."

Cameron snatched up the money, still glancing from Storm
to her mother, as if he were trying to work out a tough equation.

"My mother and I sure hope your *bowl* didn't sour!" Storm
called after him. "Get it? Milk in the bowl?"

He didn't turn around.

"What are you talking about?" Storm's mother asked.

"Quiz Bowl," Storm answered. "Let's take a break."

They walked outside and found a cool spot away from the entrance.

"About Quiz Bowl ...," Storm began. "I joined the team. That kid back there? He's on my team. Not that I'd be on his team if he had anything to say about it."

"Why would you do this?" asked her mother. "Is that where you are before you come home from school?"

Storm nodded.

"If you were so bored," her mother said sarcastically, "you should have come to me for ideas. We have a house that's never clean. You could help your father mow lawns, take on more hours here."

Storm knew it was all true. They needed the money.

"You've never talked about being on a quiz team," her mother continued. "Why now? Why, when school is almost over, would you — ?"

"Because I can get a letter," Storm said.

Her mother grew quiet. Storm didn't know if she'd understood or not.

"A varsity letter. Like the one Dad wanted and never got. I just thought ... I know it's dumb. But I thought it might help. Like he'd think his daughter belonged or something, and so he'd feel like he did too."

Storm stopped talking. Her mother wouldn't be interested in this. For years, Storm had worked hard to keep her school life as far from her home life as possible. She'd inhabited two different worlds and worked to keep the worlds apart.

She couldn't blame her mother for not taking an interest in school, when she'd done all she could to make sure her mother *wouldn't* take an interest.

Storm stared into her mom's face, looking for signs of what she was thinking. Gracie would have known. But Storm had never been able to tell what her mother was thinking. And this was no exception.

Suddenly, Storm's mom reached over and hugged her. It only lasted a few seconds. No words were spoken. Storm *couldn't* speak. She couldn't remember her no-nonsense mother hugging her, especially in a public place. Then they went back inside.

Mom's shift ended an hour before Storm's. Storm wondered how she'd make it to the end of her shift. With twenty minutes to go, the checkout lane cleared. But it hadn't cleared. Not really. Eight people stood in line, waiting. Something was holding them up.

"Next, please!" TJ shouted.

Storm gazed down the checkout lane and saw two women arguing. One of them was Lane from Quiz Bowl. Storm shook her head, wondering if God were playing a joke on her, sending both Cameron and Lane in the same day. They'd been in the store before. It wasn't like shoppers in Big Lake had many choices. They'd even come through Storm's lane on occasion, and she'd tried, unsuccessfully, to get them to laugh at her pickle facts or her turnip trivia.

But both on the same day?

"I didn't want to come in the first place!" Lane was shouting.

"Of course you didn't. You think food magically appears on the table like it does at your father's house." This came from a woman who had to be Lane's mother. She was a slightly plumper, slightly taller version of Lane.

Some of the shopping carts at the end of the line peeled off and got into other lines.

"At least at Dad's house," Lane said, "I don't have to tag along to the grocery store and dodge shopping carts from a bunch of morons."

"Shut up!" Lane's mother snarled through clenched teeth. "You hear me, you ungrateful, pitiful excuse for a daughter? Just shut — up!"

Storm looked away. Inside, she cringed. Storm had fought with her mother over clothes, over not doing enough at home, or coming in late. But her mom had never told her to shut up, never called her a pitiful excuse for a daughter.

Finally, the customer behind them got their attention, and the line moved up. Storm wanted to say something to Lane, but she was too embarrassed. "Plastic okay?" she asked Lane's mother, grateful to have something to do with her hands.

"Go ahead," Lane's mother muttered. She picked up the half-gallon of ice cream. "*This* is what you got for ice cream?"

"You said to get anything!" Lane snapped. "This falls into the category of *anything*, doesn't it?"

"Don't get smart with me!" Her mother spat out the words. "Cherry Supreme? I hate cherries. You know that. And you had to pick the most expensive brand, didn't you? Maybe that works at your father's house, but I'm a single, working mother, in case you forgot."

Lane shook her head. "Yeah. That's it. I forgot."

Storm kept her nose buried in the bags, taking extra care not to mix frozen foods with unfrozen, bread with cans.

Gracie, who was off today, claimed that she could tell a lot about a family by the food it bought. Most of what Storm had bagged for Lane and her mother would go straight to the freezer. They'd purchased everything from frozen taco dinners and frozen pizzas to frozen broccoli and frozen raspberries. No fresh meat, poultry, or fish. No fresh vegetables or fruit.

Eighteen bags of food they wouldn't have to fix.

"What's this?" Lane's mother asked.

Storm looked up to see her pointing at the bags Storm had painstakingly bagged. "Your groceries?"

Lane's mother lifted up the bag containing two cartons of eggs. "These are plastic."

Confused, Storm started to explain. "Most eggs come in plastic cartons these days, instead of the molded fiber cardboard cartons. There's this company that's teaming with a company in Austria to make clear egg boxes. And besides being cool because you can see what you're getting, they make them out of ground up plastic pop bottles. Isn't that tight? Because those things are hard to recycle."

"I don't care about that." Lane's mother set down the egg bag so hard that Storm was afraid eggs were breaking. Frowning at all eighteen shopping bags, she demanded, "I want my groceries in paper bags. I always get my groceries in paper. I never do plastic."

"But I asked you, and you said okay," Storm said.

"You most certainly did not ask!" the woman insisted.

"Actually," TJ said, "she did."

"That's ridiculous!" shouted Lane's mother. "She's lying. She never asked if I wanted plastic!"

Lane got into the act. "She never asked. I was right here, and I didn't hear her ask."

"See?" Lane's mother said triumphantly. For the first time, mother and daughter were on the same side. "I'm not going anywhere until I have my groceries in paper bags."

Storm emptied the bags, one by one, and placed each item in paper. "Good ol' paper," Storm said. "Did you know that it takes seventeen trees to make a ton of paper? The average American uses 749 pounds of paper stuff every single year."

Nobody responded, so Storm filled the silent gap. "Funny word, *paper*, don't you think? Comes from the papyrus plant that grew along the Nile in Egypt, probably when Moses was put in that basket. In Japanese, the words for *paper* and *God* are the same. Isn't that something? I guess —"

Lane interrupted. "I think I'll wait in the car."

12

The last week of classes had most kids acting crazier than usual. Teachers too. Ms. B let her classes try to paint or draw each other or anything else they felt like drawing. When Ms. B made the announcement in first period art, Jazz gave her a standing ovation.

Storm couldn't see any improvement in her dad until Wednesday, when she came home to find him out in the backyard. He was standing in the middle of the overgrown lawn. Storm hadn't noticed how long the grass had gotten.

"Hey, Dad!" she called.

He turned and gave her a weak smile. "Hello, Storm."

It was a start. *Thanks, God!* she prayed as she walked through the tall grass to get to him. "Good to see you out here."

"I'm sorry." He didn't look at her. "You and your mother suffer so when I'm like this."

"Don't worry about that," Storm said, grateful to be having any conversation with him. "Just get well." She wanted to add "now" or "fast," but she didn't.

Silence fell between them. Storm wracked her brain for something safe to break the silence with. "Can you believe how much our grass has grown?"

"It's very tall," Dad replied.

Storm could see how hard he was trying to converse with her — as hard as she was trying to converse with him. "Yeah," she went on. "Really growing." It may have been the dumbest conversation they'd ever had, but Storm felt grateful. She didn't want it to end.

"I probably looked out here every day this week," Dad said, his voice barely above a whisper. "Last week too. And each day it seemed the grass was not growing."

"I know what you mean!" Storm exclaimed. "It sneaks up on you. Like you're thinking it's stopped growing. And then one day, *poof!* It's so long. It's just like that with my hair. I'll be thinking it's not growing at all. Then one day, it's so long I can't stand it until I get it trimmed. Only it didn't really happen all of a sudden, right?"

"No. The grass grows a little at a time, until it's very long like this."

They were quiet for a while, but it was okay. Storm relaxed, and she could feel her dad doing the same. She thought about what Mick had said about why and how grass grows. "My friend Mick — you've met her — she was saying how we can water the grass and fertilize it and all. But God's the only one who can make things grow."

He didn't respond, and for a minute Storm was afraid she'd said the wrong thing. But it didn't feel wrong.

Dad leaned down and pulled up a long blade of grass. "Your friend is wise."

Storm smiled. "You don't know the half of it."

They were quiet again. Storm didn't want him to stop talking or go back inside. "Dad," she said, "how tall would grass get if you never mowed it or cut it down?"

Without hesitating, he answered, "Bamboo grows to be 130 feet tall in places."

"Bamboo? I didn't know it was a grass."

"It is the tallest grass in the world," he explained. He turned and looked directly at her. "Even bamboo does not grow overnight."

Storm knew her dad was talking about more than bamboo grass. Maybe he was trying to tell her to be patient with him, that growing out of depression didn't happen overnight either.

"I should go inside," he said. He turned toward the house.

Storm couldn't let him go. She hadn't told him about Quiz Bowl. And the competition was only three days away. "Dad?" she called after him.

He stopped and turned back. He looked so tired that she was afraid to ask him. But she might not get another chance. "I joined the Quiz Bowl team at school."

"That's good," he said, but his words sounded dry.

"There's a big Quiz Bowl competition Saturday morning. It's the last one of the year. Do you ... do you think you could come to it?"

He sucked in air through his nose. "I don't know, Storm."

"They give the winning team a trophy and everything," Storm continued, working up to what she hoped would matter to him. "And I'll get a letter. A varsity letter? You know? A school varsity letter?"

She thought she saw his eyes flicker. Then his jaw tightened, and he looked at the ground. Storm wished Gracie could have been there to read her dad's expression, to decipher his body language as he turned and trudged back inside.

The day before Quiz Bowl competition, at the end of the last practice, Mr. Stovall presented Storm with a black T-shirt that said "Quiz Bowl" on the front and "Big Lake" on the back.

It was just about the ugliest piece of clothing Storm had ever seen. "Thanks," she said, taking the shirt. "It's ... it looks like just the right size and everything."

Mr. Stovall smiled in a way that made Storm believe this whole Quiz Bowl thing meant something to him, something more than any of them knew. She'd probably never know — she was a firm believer in keeping the line between students and teachers.

Still, she realized that this was the first time she'd thought about Bones in all of this. Maybe everybody, even teachers, came with a pack full of whys and regrets, if you took the time to see past your own and wonder about theirs.

Storm was the last one to leave practice, and Mr. Stovall caught her outside the gym. "Storm, I forgot to tell you that parents are encouraged to attend the competition."

"I know, Mr. Stovall," Storm replied. "Thanks."

"Cameron never lets his parents attend," Mr. Stovall confided. "I guess they make him nervous." He grinned. "Will your parents be coming?"

Storm put on her big smile and started to answer *fasheezy!* Then something stopped her. "To tell you the truth, Mr. Stovall, I just don't know. I hope so. I think my mother might come."

"Not your father?"

Storm shrugged, then shook her head. She wanted him to come more than anything, but she and her dad hadn't talked since their conversation in the backyard. "It's not looking good right now," Storm added. "But I'm going to be praying he makes it." Even as she said it, she shot up a prayer that God would remind her to pray.

"Well, I hope he does make it, Storm. I think you'll do your parents proud."

13

The Quiz Bowl shirt turned out to be about two sizes too big for Storm — and that was the least of its problems. It was black. And plain. And so not Storm. She got talked into trying it on over her purple ruched sleeveless when the blog team met for ice cream Friday night at Sam's Sammich Shop.

"Okay. So now I'm coming to the competition for sure," Gracie teased. "I want to see Storm on stage in that shirt."

Beach Boys music blared from the jukebox, and the scent of hamburgers and fries floated around the room, which was about half full. Or half empty, depending on who was looking.

"Here you go!" Mick said, setting down a tray of her special Ice Cream à la Mick. "I think you look great in everything you wear," Mick said, as she passed out bowls and spoons.

Storm took the first bite. She loved the flavor Mick had invented. Annie's mom, Sam, owner of the shop, had added it to the official list of flavors at Sam's Sammich Shop. "Maybe I'll spill ice cream on this shirt and make it look better. What do you think, Jazz?"

Jazz closed her eyes as she downed a spoonful of the rich, colorful ice cream. "I think this ice cream could improve any shirt." She opened her eyes and leaned her elbows on the table. "You'll never guess what I did today."

"Met a guy?" Annie guessed. "Fell in love?"

Jazz shot her a raised-eyebrow look.

"Won an art award?" Mick guessed.

Storm, for once, didn't play. She eased back in the booth and thought about how lucky — no, *blessed* — she was to have friends like these. *Thanks, Lord.*

"I'm thinking Jazz is right and we'll never guess what she did today," logical Gracie commented. "So the best use of our time would be to have you tell us what we can't guess."

"I think Gracie's asking what you did today," Annie translated.

"A three-way prayer with Ty and Kendra. That's legal, right?" Jazz grinned, then closed her eyes for another long, slow spoonful of Ice Cream à la Mick.

"Legal schmegal," Gracie muttered.

"Sweet!" Annie exclaimed.

"That's so tight," Mick said. "Jazz, I love it that you guys are growing together like that."

Storm was happy for Jazz too. She loved Kendra, Jazz's little sister. And Ty was such a good kid, like Mick in a lot of ways. Jazz hadn't been a Christian very long, but her faith was more and more evident in everything she did.

But it made Storm wonder. Had *she* changed at all? She still wasn't praying like she wanted to. She still felt like smacking Cameron and Lane upside the head.

"Storm? You okay?" Mick asked the question. But Storm looked up to see all of them staring at her.

Her first reaction was to fake it and say she was fine.

But she wasn't fine. "I don't know," she admitted.

"Is it Cameron?" Gracie asked. "I heard he was causing problems at the grocery store. TJ told us all about it. I can imagine he's not your biggest fan on the Quiz Bowl team."

"Not a lot of competition for that role — my biggest fan," Storm joked. She grinned at Mick. "Mick got me thinking that there had to be a reason Cameron is so bent on making my life miserable and booting me off that team, but I haven't figured it out yet."

"You know he's got an older sister at Harvard or Yale or somewhere like that, right?" Jazz offered.

"Oooh! So maybe," Annie began, her blue eyes big and bright, "maybe she's perfect! And, like, Cameron's afraid he won't measure up. And he doesn't like females who are smarter than he is?"

"Or maybe," Gracie said, apparently trying to mimic Annie's bounciness, but not quite pulling it off, "he's got a thing against Mayan princesses? Or girls who wear bright colors? Or — "

Annie poised her spoonful of ice cream in launch mode, aimed at Gracie. "Wonder how funny you'd be with ice cream in your face," she teased.

Mick came between them. "You guys." She turned to Storm. "I think what Gracie's trying to say — in her own Gracie way — is that we really don't know what's up with Cameron. Sorry if I made you think I did, or anything."

"You didn't, Mick," Storm said. She wanted to explain, but she wasn't sure what she was feeling herself. "You just thought about Cameron, and that was something I hadn't even thought to think about. Does that make sense?"

"No," Jazz said.

"Of course it doesn't make sense to you, Jazz," Storm replied. "You've changed since you became a Christian. In a good way."

Jazz wrinkled her nose. "What?"

"*You've* changed. You're praying with your brother and sister. If I've changed at all," Storm complained, "I've gotten worse."

"No way," Gracie said. "Like you could get worse."

Storm reached across the table to punch Gracie's arm. She knew her friend was kidding, and she appreciated it. But she wasn't going to stop here. "Why is it that I feel like I'm snapping at people more, telling more 'white lies,' and having more bad thoughts than before I was a Christian?" Her throat burned from holding back tears, but it felt good to get the truth out. "What's wrong with me?"

Annie and Mick got up from the table to give Storm a hug.

"Nothing's wrong with you!" Annie insisted, her eyes filling with tears. "You're perfect just like you are!"

"Storm, this is way cool!" Mick sounded sincerely excited, and Storm knew Mick never faked things like this. "This proves that you've changed, Storm. Don't you get it?"

"It's cool that I'm messing up more?" Storm asked.

"You're not," Gracie explained. "You just didn't see things before. You didn't have the lights on. Never a pretty picture once the light goes on."

Storm struggled to understand. "The lights on?"

"You didn't notice the sins before," Mick explained. "They didn't bother you then. But they bother you now because God's Spirit is in you. See? Way cool."

"Really?" Storm shivered thinking about it. She tried to remember what it had been like before she'd believed in Christ.

"I don't know much about it," Jazz admitted. "But it makes sense. I feel like you do all the time, Storm."

"Me too," Gracie admitted.

Storm felt on the verge of getting this. "Do you really think I'm growing?" Storm asked.

"So you want proof?" Gracie said.

"Not proof exactly, although that would be cool." Storm turned to Jazz. "Did you really pray with Ty and Kendra?"

Jazz grinned. "Well, we talked to God together. Not sure everybody would call it prayer. Ty thanked God for coming up with a game like baseball, and he prayed the Indians would stop trading away their best players and would get some solid pitching."

"No kidding," Mick muttered.

"And Kendra talked to God a long time about everything, from toenails to the color green," Jazz continued.

They laughed. Kendra had Down syndrome and the freedom to say whatever popped into her head. Storm loved that about her.

"How about you?" Annie asked. "What did you pray for?"

Jazz's dark eyes narrowed. "You guys, of course."

"That's so nice, Jazz," Mick said.

"You *do* need a lot of prayer," Jazz teased.

"True dat," Storm agreed.

"We could pray together now," Mick suggested. "Storm, you want to pray for your competition tomorrow?"

"Totally," Storm answered. She closed her eyes, even though she knew she didn't have to. Chances were, her friends would just look down at the table, not to draw attention to themselves. But Storm needed to focus on God.

At the next table, two boys, probably in elementary school, were arguing. They were loud, fighting over fries, calling each other names. Storm squeezed her eyes shut, hoping she could shut out their words and tune into God instead.

Mick started. She talked to God as if he were sitting at the table with them. Maybe he was, Storm decided. "Help Storm tomorrow, God," Mick prayed. "And clue her in so she knows you're right there with her."

Gracie prayed Storm would have a clear head for the competition.

Annie prayed Storm would actually enjoy herself and have fun. She prayed for Storm's dad too.

Jazz prayed something short, but her voice was muffled and Storm couldn't be sure she caught it. Somehow, though, the exact words didn't matter.

Storm went next. Her words came out slowly at first. Then they tumbled out, like they were exiting her heart, instead of her mouth. "Please help my dad get through this depression. And if it will help him to be at the competition, then get him there. Okay? And about the competition, Lord, help me not to mess up, and not to be selfish or full of myself there. I'd like to pray for Edward too. He gets so nervous. And maybe it would be good if Lane's mom *and* dad showed up for her. And help Cameron see that there's more to life than what he sees ahead of him now."

Storm stopped praying. She realized that the boys at the next table were shouting at each other. She hadn't even heard them until she stopped praying.

Gracie and Jazz were laughing.

At first, Storm thought they were laughing at her, the way she prayed. But she knew they wouldn't do that. "What?" she asked.

Then Annie joined them, laughing harder than Gracie and Jazz put together. "Sweet!"

Storm turned to Mick. But even Mick the Munch looked like she was fighting off a laugh. "Storm, don't you get it?"

Storm had no idea what they were talking about. Or laughing about. "Get what?"

"If you needed proof," Gracie said, "I guess you've got it."

"What are talking about?" Storm demanded.

Mick put her arm around Storm's shoulder and leaned in. "Storm, you were praying."

"Yeah?" Storm didn't think that was proof that she was growing in Christ. Even when she hadn't known much about Jesus, she'd prayed. Or tried to, anyway.

Mick squeezed Storm's shoulder. "You were praying ... for Cameron."

For a second, Storm couldn't breathe. "I — I *was!*" she exclaimed.

"No way you would have prayed for him a week ago," Gracie observed.

"Or a day ago," Annie said.

Storm thought about it. They were right. "Unbelievable," she muttered, amazed. She hadn't even made herself do it. It had just been there, something God put in her heart. Something the Spirit must have brought out.

"Entirely believable," Gracie corrected.

"*You* finish it!" one of the boys at the table next to them shouted.

They all turned to see the two boys who'd been fighting since they'd gotten their fries. The blond-headed kid sat back in the booth, his arms crossed in front of him.

The other boy shoved the plate of gross leftover fries across the table. "No way!" he screamed. "*You* started it. *You* finish it!"

"Exactly!" Gracie said.

"What?" Storm didn't get it ... again.

"Mick, give Storm the verse you're using for next week's blog," Gracie said.

Mick's smile took up her whole face. "'Being confident of this,'" she began, obviously quoting the new verse, "'that he who began a good work in you will carry it on to completion until the day of Christ Jesus.' Get it?"

Storm got it. God was still working on her. He started it, and he'd finish it.

The two boys stopped arguing and turned to stare at the table full of praying females.

Gracie waved at them. "Don't worry, guys. He's not finished with you, either."

14

"What nut is the oldest — ?"

Storm buzzed in. "Almonds!"

"Correct." The moderator, who wore a pin-striped suit, green scarf, and Pradas, smiled at Storm.

Storm had gotten off to a slow start, and her team had fallen behind. They'd lost the first category, math. And thanks to her, they'd lost the English category too. Even though she'd known the answers, she kept buzzing in too early and answering the wrong question.

Cameron had been ready to tape her hands behind her back.

But things had gotten better.

"Cranberries are one of just three major fruits indigenous to North America. Name —"

"Concord grapes and blueberries!" Storm shouted, a second after she hit her buzzer. Then she wished she had it back. The moderator might have been about to ask *where* cranberries originated or maybe something else about cranberries.

"That is correct," said the moderator.

Storm and her team let out a collective sigh.

For the hundredth time, Storm glanced out at the skimpy crowd. Students didn't turn out for Quiz Bowl the way they did for basketball. There hadn't been a Quiz Bowl pep rally.

Still, the whole blog team had turned out. They took up the front row and smiled up at her, cheering every point.

Storm scanned the door, the back of the gym, the side door. Still no sign of her dad or her mom. She'd been sure her mom would show up, at least.

"Volcanoes," Cameron said, his voice totally calm.

Storm hadn't even heard the question. "Way to go, Cameron!" she said. She'd cheered every right answer he and Lane had given, even though they hadn't returned the favor. Edward did, though. And he'd gotten two math questions right to keep them in the competition.

Storm made herself focus. She prayed that God would help her pay attention. Then she remembered to pray for her teammates too.

The final round was a team effort. "You'll have three minutes to confer with your teammates on the same question as your opponents," the moderator explained. "I'll offer one point for each right answer and subtract one point for each wrong answer. You may use the pad and pencil in front of you."

Storm's teammates didn't pick up the pencil, so she did. When she glanced up from the little pad of paper, she thought she was seeing things. There stood her parents, alone in the back of the auditorium. She watched as they walked to the front row and took seats next to the blog team.

Thanks, God.

"Ready?" The moderator waited for a nod from both captains. "Very good. List familiar names that normally have the words *the Great* appended to them. Begin."

Storm wrote as fast as she could, jotting down her own ideas in between recording the ideas of her teammates. The

Sharks were behind in overall points. They needed almost twice as many points as their opponents from this final round.

Lane was on a roll: Pompey the Great. Otto I, the Great. John Paul II, the Great. Ivan the Great. Peter the Great. Catherine the Great.

Edward contributed his list that sounded like people Storm had heard about in the Bible: Xerxes the Great. Ramses the Great. Darius the Great. Herod the Great.

Cameron came up with the most names: Alexander the Great. Casimir the Great. Charles the Great. Constantine the Great. Louis the Great. Theodosius the Great. William I, the Great, Yu the Great. Sejong the Great. The Great Khan. Frederick the Great. Cyrus the Great.

Storm had already written down some of the names her teammates shouted at her. But her mind had moved in a different direction: The Great Houdini. Jackie Gleason — the one her dad called "The Great One." Her dad loved Wayne Gretzky, some hockey player, and Storm was sure Gretzky was called "The Great One" by hockey fans.

She added other "greats" too: The Great Gatsby, The Great Santini, The Great Pumpkin from the *Peanuts* comic strip she and her dad read together, Gonzo the Great, and Sheila the Great — other characters from her childhood.

"Time," said the moderator. "I'll give you sixty seconds to look over your list and make sure you have only the names you want to present. Remember that each wrong name will be a penalty point."

"The Great Pumpkin?" Lane cried, reading over Storm's shoulder. "Gonzo? You can't put Gonzo!"

Edward was grinning. "The question didn't say they had to be real people, Lane."

"But Muppets?" Lane snapped.

Cameron snatched the list from Storm's hands. His gaze moved down the paper, as he muttered, "Great Santini? Great Gatsby? Who's Sheila the Great?"

"We need these points," Edward said.

Cameron frowned down at Storm.

Storm shrugged.

Cameron looked to Lane. After a second, she shrugged too.

"Time," called the moderator. She had the other team read off their names first. They got a lot of the same names as the Sharks, plus a few Storm's side didn't have: *Ashoka the Great of India, Justinian the Great, Tigranes the Great of Armenia.*

"Big Lake, it's your turn." The moderator waited.

Finally, Cameron seemed to make up his mind. He read out the list. The whole list. Even when the audience burst into laughter at the Great Pumpkin, he kept reading, ending with Gonzo the Great.

Laugher filled the auditorium.

Storm glanced at the first row to make sure her parents were still there. They were. And they were laughing. It felt so good to see her dad laugh.

The moderator consulted the judges. Then she announced, "All names on both sides are approved and accepted."

Annie jumped up from her seat and shouted, "Go, Big Lake!"

"Which brings us," the moderator continued, "to a tie score."

Storm couldn't believe it. They'd made an amazing comeback.

Edward was cheering, pounding Storm on the back. Lane and Cameron smiled and shook their heads in disbelief.

"Gonzo," Lane muttered. "Who would have thought?"

"We'll decide the match with a toss-up question," the moderator explained. "I'll ask one question. The first person to buzz in must answer for his or her team. If you are correct, you win the match. If you are incorrect, your opponents will go home with the trophy."

Storm looked at the people sitting in the front row, and she felt overwhelmingly grateful. Her friends had supported her all along. Her mother had understood about the Quiz Bowl and the letter. And her father had battled back his depression enough to come and see her compete.

The gym grew still as the moderator stepped closer to the mike. "Name the tallest grass in the world."

Storm hit the buzzer. "Bamboo!" she shouted. She grinned out at her dad. He'd been the one to tell her that. Her dad! She wanted everybody to know that the answer came from her dad. "My dad says bamboo can grow to 130 feet or taller," she explained.

Storm felt Cameron's hand on her arm, warning her to stop and not risk misinformation.

But she couldn't stop. She wasn't talking to the moderator any longer. She was talking to her dad. "Bamboo grows a little bit at a time, just like everything in life."

"Storm?" Edward whispered, sounding concerned.

"You can water and feed the bamboo all you want. But everybody knows that God's the only one who can make things grow."

Somebody gasped. It might have been Lane.

Storm realized what she'd said ... about God. She hadn't planned it, but it was true. She gazed up at the moderator.

How could they not see how true it all was. She saw it.
Finally. Growing wasn't up to her. That was God's job.

"Thank you, Big Lake," said the moderator. "You are our
new Quiz Bowl winner. Congratulations."

The auditorium burst into cheers. Storm hugged all three
of her teammates. Mr. Stovall came up on stage and received
the trophy, while Storm ran down to her parents.

"Nice speech," said her dad, grinning.

"Yeah?" She smiled at him and saw her real dad peeking
through, finding his way out again. As soon as she got her
varsity letter, she'd sew it on her dad's sweater. He'd earned it.

"You should go celebrate with your friends," said her mom,
putting her arm around Dad.

Storm hesitated.

"Go," her father agreed. "I have work to do."

Storm's mother smiled. "Your father began mowing our
lawn early this morning."

"Way to go, Dad!" Storm exclaimed.

"It's not finished yet," he admitted.

Storm felt a surge of gratitude as she watched her parents
walk away.

She turned to her friends. "Did you hear him?" she
asked, her voice cracking. Her throat felt so tight that it was
amazing words could get out at all.

Mick hugged her. The rest of them looked as choked up as
she felt.

Storm believed she had the best friends in the whole world.
And, thanks to God, they were all still growing, even Mick.

God wasn't finished with them yet.

Internet Safety by Michaela

People aren't always what they seem at first, like wolves in sheep's clothing. Chat rooms, blogs, and other places online can be fun ways to meet all kinds of people with all kinds of interests. But be aware and cautious. Here are some tips to help keep you safe while surfing the web, keeping a blog, chatting online, and writing e-mails.

- Never give out personal information such as your address, phone number, parents' work addresses or phone numbers, or the name and address of your school without your parents' or guardian's permission. It's okay to talk about your likes and dislikes, but keep private information just that—private.

- Before you agree to meet someone in person, first check with your parents or guardian to make sure it's okay. A safe way to meet for the first time is to bring a parent or guardian with you.

- You might be tempted to send a picture of yourself to new friends you've met online. Just in case your acquaintance is not who you think they are, check with your parent or guardian before you hit send.

- If you feel uncomfortable by angry, threatening, or other types of e-mails or posts addressed to you, tell your parent or guardian immediately.

- Before you promise to call a new friend on the telephone, talk to your parent or guardian first.

- Remember that just because you might read about something or someone online doesn't mean the information is true. Sometimes people say cruel or untruthful things just to be mean.

- If someone writes creepy posts, report him or her to the blog or website owner.

Following these tips will help keep you safe while you hang out online. If you're careful, you can learn a lot and meet tons of new people.

Subject: Michaela Jenkins

Age: 13 on May 19, 7th grade at Big Lake Middle School
Hair/Eyes: Dark brown hair/Brown eyes
Height: 5'

"Mick the Munch" is content and rooted in her relationship with Christ. She lives with her stepsis, Grace Doe, in the blended family of Gracie's dad and Mick's mom. She's a tomboy, an avid Cleveland Indians fan, and the only girl on her school's baseball team. A computer whiz, Mick keeps *That's What You Think!* up and running. She also helps out at Sam's Sammich Shop and manages to show her friends what deep faith looks like.

Subject: Grace Doe

Age: 15 on August 19, sophomore
Hair/Eyes: Blonde hair/Hazel eyes
Height: 5' 5"

Grace doesn't think she is cute at all. The word "average" was meant for her. She dresses in neutral colors and camouflage to blend in. Grace does not wear makeup. She prefers to observe life rather than participate in it. A bagger at a grocery store, only her close friends and family can get away with calling her "Gracie." She is part of a blended family and lives with her dad and stepmom, two stepsiblings, and two half brothers. Her mother's job frequently keeps her out of town.

Subject: Annie Lind

Age: 16 on October 1, sophomore
Hair/Eyes: Auburn hair/Blue eyes
Height: 5' 10"

Annie desperately wants guys to admire and like her. She is boy-crazy and thinks she always has to be in love. She considers herself to be an expert in matters of the heart. Annie takes being popular for granted because she has always been well-liked. She loves and admires her mom. Her dad was killed in a plane crash when Annie was two months old. Annie helps out at Sam's Sammich Shop, her mom's restaurant. She can be self-centered, though without being selfish.

Subject: Jasmine Fletcher

Age: 15 on July 13, freshman
Hair/Eyes: Black hair/Brown eyes
Height: 5' 6"

Jasmine is an artist who feels that no one, especially her art teacher and parents, understands her art. She is African American, and has great fashion sense, without being trendy. Her parents are quite well-to-do, and they won't let Jasmine get a job. She has a younger brother and a sister who has Down syndrome. She also had a brother who was killed in a drive-by shooting in the old neighborhood when Jazz was one.

Subject: Storm Novello

Age: 14 on September 1, freshman
Hair/Eyes: Brown hair/Dark brown eyes
Height: 5' 2"

Storm doesn't realize how pretty she is. She wishes she had blonde hair. She is Mayan/Mestisa, and claims to be a Mayan princess. Storm always needs to be the center of attention and doesn't let on how smart she is. She dresses in bright, flouncy clothing, and wears too much makeup. Storm is a completely different person around her parents. She changes into her clothes and puts her makeup on after leaving for school. Her parents are very loving, though they have little money.

1

THAT'S WHAT YOU THINK!
By Jane
AUGUST 28
SUBJECT: BP GIRL

Ever notice how right before some people go off or blow or explode, their eyelids flicker? Their lips squeeze together. Then those tendons in the neck turn into rope strands? No? You never noticed that?

Well, neither did poor Bouncy Perky Girl. Right before history class, she took it upon her perky self to demonstrate a new cheer for us. Bones was behind his desk already. (You remember my history teacher, Bones, as in "Dry as . . .") So BP Girl (Bouncy Perky) was midair when the bell rang. She couldn't stop because she was just getting to the part about Typical High fight-fight-fighting. Bones pushed himself up from his desk and walked over to BP Girl. She flashed him a Typical High cheerleader smile and moved into the win-win-win part of the cheer.

I saw what was coming a mile off, or at least fifteen feet off, from my seat in the back. Bones' eyelids twitched. His lips got even thinner.

It was like watching a train streaking toward a puppy on the tracks. Bones's neck turned into rope strands, and still BP Girl cheered on. I imagined the toe of a cowboy boot aimed and ready to deliver a blow to the puppy.

Bones screamed at BP Girl and ordered her to take her seat. She was totally surprised. You could have scraped her off the blackboard. I actually felt sorry for Bouncy Perky Girl.

Grace Doe sat back and studied the computer screen. The blog entry wasn't bad. She'd have time to edit it before uploading to her website. She could answer a couple of the emails and respond to comments, then post those too. But first, she wanted to write about Jazz.

. . . .

THAT'S WHAT YOU THINK!
SUBJECT: JAZZ

There's this girl at Typical High, smooth and deep as Jazz. Lithe, with wild, black hair. She's got a moody wit that's mostly wasted at our school. Yesterday at lunch, Steroid Boy was bragging about becoming a vegetarian. I could tell he was trying to impress Jazz. But she kept eating from a box of animal crackers. When Steroid Boy finally stopped talking, Jazz said, "I'd offer you one of my animal crackers, but I couldn't live with myself if I brought on a crisis of faith for you." It was classic! But Steroid Boy just nodded, like he was agreeing with her.

I've been observing Jazz since school started. She doodles in her notebook margins. Cool sketches — kids, teachers, or just designs. I think she's the real deal.

Gracie had been blogging — keeping an open journal, or "web log," on the Internet — for almost two months. And still, the only person who knew the identity of "Jane" was Gracie's little stepsis, Michaela. The only reason Mick the Munch knew about the blog was that Gracie needed the computer munchkin to set up the website and keep it running.

The door to Gracie's bedroom slammed open. She lunged to shut off the computer. But it was just Mick, in jeans and a Cleveland Indians baseball shirt. Her dark brown ponytail stuck out through the hole in her Indians cap. "Gracie, hurry up! Luke's waiting. You're going to make us late for school."

Gracie's stepbrother, Luke, was a senior at Big Lake High — blog name, "Typical High" — where Gracie was a sophomore. Mick's middle school was right next door, and Luke, under protest, usually drove them both to school.

"Coming," Gracie muttered, logging off.

Mick came over to the desk. "Did you get your bill from the server, Gracie?"

Gracie felt the familiar tightening in her stomach. "I said I'd handle it, Mick."

She was two weeks late on the payment for her website. She could pay it on Saturday, when she got paid for bagging groceries at Big Lake Foods. Until then, she just couldn't think about it.

She got up, ran her fingers through her short blonde hair, slid her cell into her backpack, and slipped into her flip-flops. Khaki pants, army green T-shirt — all set. One of the benefits of being invisible at school was that nobody noticed your wardrobe.

Luke had the motor running in his ghetto Ford. "About time," he called, shoving the passenger door open for Gracie. It didn't work from the outside. Mick hopped into the back.

"My fault, Luke," Gracie admitted.

Luke shrugged, turned up the radio, and headed down the drive. "Well, next time, I'm leaving without you."

Gracie believed him. Luke could be a pain. He treated her like she was five instead of fifteen, especially when he was around his girlfriend. Next year he'd be off to Ohio State, and Gracie figured he wouldn't give her a single thought. She was just the stepsister. Gracie had refused to attend the wedding three years ago when her dad married Lisa, Luke and Mick's mom. She'd hated the idea of a "blended family." Like all you had to do was dump kids from different gene pools into a blender and come up with a smoothie.

Since her parents' divorce, Gracie had been getting along okay living with her dad and seeing her mom whenever she bounced into town. Then, just like that, she'd gone from being the only child of Barry and Victoria Doe (the youngest and the oldest child) to being the middle child of Barry and Lisa Doe.

She liked Lisa. Luke could drive her postal, but Mick was impossible not to like. Still, Gracie couldn't shake the feeling that she was "odd man out" in the Doe household, which now included one-year-old twins.

Luke found a spot in the A parking lot, right between Mick's middle school and Big Lake High. A couple of senior girls pulled up next to them. He checked his hair in the rearview, even though it was too short to get messed up. Gracie had to admit that Luke Jenkins was good-looking.

Mick dipped out fast. "Thanks for the ride, Luke! I'm going to Ty's after school. Bye, Gracie!" Then she ran to catch up with Ty Fletcher, her baseball buddy.

Luke opened his door and called out to the girls who had climbed out of the car next to his: "Wait up!"

They stopped, smiled back at him, and waited.

"What about Jessica?" Gracie asked. But she'd been rooting for more than a month for Luke to dump his girlfriend. She was too fake for Luke.

Luke got out of the car. "Hey, I'm not married. Or dead." Then he walked off between the blondes.

Gracie trudged into Big Lake High alone, imagining that she was as invisible as the humid air that pressed in on her from all sides.

Inside, the halls buzzed. A senior couple leaned against the locker next to Gracie's. Behind her, two girls were arguing. A group of guys blocking the hall erupted in an explosion of laughter.

Gracie took out her recording notebook, leaned against her locker, and observed. This was where she got material for her blog. Three lockers down, Steroid Boy, whose real name was Bryce, was trying out his vegetarian routine on an unsuspecting freshman.

"Goes against my consciousness to eat meat," he told her.

Gracie jotted in her notebook: "Pupils dilated. He blinks four times. He touches his forehead twice. Steroid Boy is lying."

She couldn't even remember when or where she'd learned behavior signs like these. She'd read dozens of books about human behavior. But most of her real insights came from simply watching people. And taking notes.

Someone bumped her arm and kept walking. It didn't surprise her. Who says "Excuse me" to an invisible woman? Grace Doe had always been the kind of person nobody noticed or remembered. She'd come to accept that role and learned to take advantage of it.

Gracie looked up to see Annie Lind — blog name, Bouncy Perky Girl. Even without her brown and blue cheerleading uniform, Annie looked like a cheerleader — tall and bouncy, auburn hair, and giant blue eyes. She was surrounded by four hotties competing for her attention.

"True dat!" Annie cried, arm-punching Jared, Big Lake's star quarterback. "The boy's got game."

To be honest, Gracie had to admit Annie had never said a mean word to her. Then again, Gracie and Annie had hardly said any words to each other their whole freshman year.

Gracie waited until the bell rang to go to her first-hour class. Most kids took art their freshman year, which was probably why Gracie had waited until now to enroll as a sophomore. No one would ever accuse Grace Doe of following the crowd.

She floated to the back of the room, keeping her notebook handy. Gracie planned to be a writer, not an artist. Forcing herself to keep an online journal had been the best thing she'd ever done for her writing career. Her art, on the other hand, would never progress past the stick-figure stage, no matter how much she drew.

The art teacher, Ms. Biederman, couldn't have looked less like an artist if she'd tried. Kempt. That's the word Gracie had used in her notebook. The woman was entirely too neat and clean for art.

"Class, please?" Ms. B's voice grated on Gracie's nerves. "Today, paint something in this room. Make it representational. I want to be able to tell what you've drawn."

Chairs screeched as kids moved to the art cupboard. Most of them took the smallest poster board they could find, then pulled chairs around Ms. B's desk, where she'd set up a flower arrangement.

Gracie waited until the room settled. Then she sat down in front of the wastebasket, her back to the room, and tried to draw the rippled army green waste can.

Ms. Biederman spent most of the class time shutting people up instead of instructing them in how to draw. "People, please!" she whined. "Your mouths should not be moving!"

It took Gracie only fifteen minutes to draw the wastebasket, which ended up looking a lot like a barrel. She stood up and glanced around the room until she spotted Jazz, also known as Jasmine Fletcher. Nobody called her Jazz except Gracie, on the blog. Jasmine stood behind an easel in the back of the room. Her poster board looked three times the size of everyone else's.

Jazz didn't seem to notice as Gracie eased behind her. On the white board, red, blue, and yellow lines intersected, rose and fell. Gracie had never liked abstract art. She didn't "get" most of it. But this was different. Jazz had turned the poster board into something else. Gracie couldn't look away.

"Jasmine? What are you *doing*?" Ms. Biederman's voice sliced through Gracie's thoughts. She'd been so into Jazz's painting that she hadn't seen the art teacher creep up.

"What do you mean?" Jazz asked, her voice calm and controlled. But Gracie saw her jaw tighten, as if she were biting nails. Her body leaned away from their art teacher. Gracie recognized signs of anger when she saw them.

"What do I mean?" Ms. B's voice tripled in volume.

Storm Rising

Softcover • ISBN 0-310-71096-0

Nobody knows the real Storm... not even Storm! The center of attention wherever she goes, Storm Novelo is impetuous, daring, loud—and a phony. Convinced that no one would like her inner brainiac, she hides her genius behind her public airhead.

Grace Under Pressure

Softcover • ISBN 0-310-71263-7

Gracie's always been good at handling everything herself, but pressures at school and personal disappointments prove almost more than she can bear in this fifth book in the Blog On series. Will she learn to share her burdens with God and with her friends before she cracks?

Upsetting Annie

Softcover • ISBN 0-310-71264-5

Annie has a great life. She loves her girlfriends, never lacks for guy friends, and she's a cheerleader too. But her confidence is shaken when her cousin from Paris, France, moves in. Shawna is funny, cute, and a talented cheerleader. Soon Shawna is the center of attention— and Annie's not. How can she banish jealousy before it ruins her life?

Jazz Off-Key

Softcover • ISBN 0-310-71265-3

When Jazz gets her big break—her own one-woman art show— she's ecstatic. But when Kendra, her specialneeds sister, unintentionally ruins the paintings by adding color to make them happier, Jazz loses it ... and her rage just keeps growing. Will she ever learn to manage her anger?

Available now at your local bookstore!

faiThGirLz!
2 corinthians 4:18

Inner Beauty, Outward Faith

Book 1 **Sophie's World**. . . . . Softcover . . . ISBN 0-310-70756-0

Book 2 **Sophie's Secret**. . . . . Softcover . . . ISBN 0-310-70757-9

Book 3 **Sophie and the Scoundrels** . Softcover . . . ISBN 0-310-70758-7

Book 4 **Sophie's Irish Showdown**. . . Softcover . . . ISBN 0-310-70759-5

Book 5 **Sophie's First Dance?** . . . . . . Softcover . . . ISBN 0-310-70760-9

Book 6 **Sophie's Stormy Summer**. . . Softcover . . . ISBN 0-310-70761-7

Book 7 **Sophie Breaks the Code** . . . . Softcover . . . ISBN 0-310-71022-7

Book 8 **Sophie Tracks a Thief** . . . . . Softcover . . . ISBN 0-310-71023-5

Book 9 **Sophie Flakes Out**. . . . . Softcover . . . ISBN 0-310-71024-3

Book 10 **Sophie Loves Jimmy**. . . . . . . Softcover . . . ISBN 0-310-71025-1

Book 11 **Sophie Loses the Lead** . . . . . Softcover . . . ISBN 0-310-71026-X

Book 12 **Sophie's Encore**. . . . . Softcover . . . ISBN 0-310-71027-8

Available now at your local bookstore!

 ZONDERkidz™

faiThGirLz!

2 corinthians 4:18

Inner Beauty, Outward Faith

Faithgirlz! Journal

Spiral • ISBN 0-310-71190-8

The questions in this new Faithgirlz!™ journal focus on your life, family, friends, and future. Because your favorites and issues seem to change every day, the same set of questions are repeated in each section. Includes quizzes to promote reflection and stickers to add fun!

NIV Faithgirlz! Backpack Bible

Periwinkle Italian Duo-Tone™ • ISBN 0-310-71012-X

The full NIV text in a handy size for girls on the go—for ages 8 and up.

Available now at your local bookstore

ZONDERkidz™

faiThGirLz!™
2 corinthians 4:18

Inner Beauty, Outward Faith

Visit **faithgirlz.com**—
it's the place for girls ages 8-12!

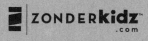